Loneliness and other Lovers

Ann Oosthuizen

Sheba Feminist Publishers

Published 1981 by Sheba Feminist Publishers, 488 Kingsland Road,
London E8 4AE
2nd Impression 1982
Copyright ©Ann Oosthuizen 1981
ISBN 0 907179 08 8
Cover design by An Dekker
Typeset in Garamond 10/11 by Range Left Photosetters (TU), 30
Clerkenwell Close, London EC1
Printed and bound by A Wheaton & Co Ltd, Exeter

With thanks to The Arts Council of Great Britain for financial
assistance

For Claire and Jill and Ali and Michele, Tina and Stef and Stephanie — and all the other women who started me off.

Summer

Chapter One

She emerged out of the darkness at Regent's Park tube station, as she had been instructed. She was carrying a small suitcase and the map which Christopher had drawn for her. 'You can have my room when I leave,' he had said, 'at least for a fortnight. I'll fix it up for you. Just write what time you think you will be arriving,' and he had drawn the map on the back of an envelope which she had provided, grabbing the nearest piece of paper she could find.

She looked at it now, turning it round so that the street in front of her would correspond to the one marked Marylebone Road at the bottom of the drawing. That's right, keep going until the lights, cross over and walk up the Outer Circle, the park on your left until you get to Chester Gate. She was unused to the city, knew only its main landmarks, Trafalgar Square, Piccadilly Circus, from those days she and Stephen had come up to town for exhibitions or the theatre. Then Stephen always held the map and she followed him through the labyrinth of underground passages like an adventurous rabbit. She had no idea how the place fitted together or what it would mean to say 'I live in Camden Town', or how far away that was from the West End or any of the main railway stations. Christopher had said that the mews was near Regent's Park, that it was a squat (what would that be like?) and that there were four people living there at the moment.

London got very dirty in this heat, she thought, looking at her hands which were already streaked with black just from touching the stair rail. There was a man selling ice-creams and cold drinks on the corner as she crossed over towards the park. As she looked through the gates she could see formal flower beds with bright red geraniums, some planted in stone urns, straight tarred paths with people and dogs. She crossed over again to be closer to the houses so that she wouldn't miss the turning. They seemed very grand, colonnaded with large windows. The street lights were held up by stone women in flowing draperies. Railings and dusty laurel bushes kept her away from front doors and bright interiors, but she could read the street signs, Cambridge Terrace, she must be near now, and suddenly, two corners later, she turned into the mews, a cobbled cul-de-sac, empty except for a large ginger cat who stared at her from a garage roof.

There was no reply when she rang the bell at number five. The house was as quiet as the courtyard it faced onto. She put down her suitcase and sat on it. What should she do? It was as she had expected, she supposed, it was too much to hope that things would go well now after so much had fallen away. In April she had moved a few possessions to her mother's home after Stephen had announced that he intended to apply for a divorce. By then, of course, it wasn't a shock, merely the next logical step after that Sunday afternoon when he had told her that he was in love with a lecturer in the History Department and that it was serious this time. This time. Over the years there had been so many other women that she had developed a kind of protective shell, the bright, clever wife of the Professor of Engineering, who entertained lavishly and wore amazing clothes. She had never felt secure, but he still introduced her as 'my wife' and she clung to the status it provided at formal university occasions, covering herself, out of fear of the alternatives, with the shreds of dignity allowed to women who shared a legal bed with those men who had found their way via Oxford or Cambridge or Edinburgh to teach the most promising students of each generation.

How long should she wait? She looked at her watch and calculated that if she hung on for an hour she could still catch the 4.45 back to Winchester and be with her mother in good time to ensure that there would be a place for her at the dinner table. Contingency plans. She had been making a lot of them lately. At forty-three it isn't easy to start again. She had qualifications, of course, had even done quite a bit of teaching when there was need for money for Jeremy's music lessons or a new car. What she wanted now was to get right away and London seemed big enough to hide in.

Her mother had offered her a home in Winchester, but she could imagine herself growing old there quickly, falling into patterns which would be as iron moulded as the very railings that she had passed today. She would be dependent on other people, her mother, even Stephen, and in her anger at him she needed to be more than an object of pity, more than a piece of his life that he had thrown away. Her mother represented old age to her, and she wasn't ready for that yet. No, London was where she could perhaps find a job that would give her enough to live on and a world of people who did not know that she was poor Jean, the wife of that randy professor who couldn't keep his hands off young female lecturers, especially if they were pretty. She had had enough of those kindly, knowing questions: 'Well Jean, how are you finding yourself these days? Keeping busy? You must come over to tea one afternoon. Wait until the boys are back at school and then we can have a nice quiet, cosy chat, just the two of us.'

That was enough. She hadn't come to London to wallow in self-pity. Perhaps if no one came soon, she could leave her suitcase at Waterloo and go to the new exhibition at the Hayward. She had been meaning to see it, and it would be fun even if she did have to return to Winchester that evening and maybe there would be time for a film as well. Already the day seemed brighter. She would just wait another – at this moment a young man on a bicycle came swooping around the corner of the mews, skidding to a stop with such suddenness that he almost fell at her feet.

Jean laughed: 'Are you all right?' He was extraordinarily beautiful, his face open, as if he had spent a lot of time out of doors, his long hair a mass of untidy curls which he had tied back with a strip of leather.

'Hello,' he said, propping his bicycle against the wall. 'I'm sorry I'm late. I'll just put my bicycle away and then let you in.' He had a key for number three as well, but when he opened it, it turned out to be merely the entrance to a flight of stairs onto which he quickly swung his bike. He had long thin legs in brown corduroy trousers and on his feet were large, soft, hand-made leather boots.

'You must be Jean,' he went on as he fiddled with keys and led the way up a second flight of stairs. 'We got your letter today. I'm Don. I live here, at least for now, and I said I'd let you in, though I just rushed out to do some shopping.' He carried a leather school bag over one shoulder. 'I'm usually here, you see. I work here most of the time.'

She followed him into a narrow room. The two windows facing her were framed by creepers and a soft, green light filtered through them — it was very quiet. She had not imagined London to be so quiet. Under the first window there was a carpeted sitting area with a low table made out of bricks and a piece of polished wood. On it was one of those plants which seem to fall out of their pots and die in the middle. Also a very full ashtray and two empty coffee cups.

Although the room was narrow, it was quite long. A stove stood under the other window, and a low cupboard against the far wall was covered with a jumble of dirty plates, margarine, nescafe, milk cartons, breadcrumbs and an open marmite jar. Don had disappeared down a passage, but reappeared with a kettle. 'I'm making coffee, do you want some?'

'Yes please.' She sat down with her back against the wall and let the room wash over her. It was a busy, messy place, it spoke of meals cooked in a hurry and eaten hastily, lots of disparate lives. Yesterday's *Evening Standard* lay on the floor next to some pamphlets about troops out of Ireland.

'You know Christopher don't you?' asked Don as he gathered two mugs from the cupboard to whisk them off somewhere to wash them.

'Yes,' she answered when he returned, 'he and my son,

Jeremy, were at university together. He was visiting last week and he said he was leaving his room and he'd ask if I could use it for a couple of weeks. I wanted to come to London to look for a room and to go to the women's liberation conference — is it all right if I stay?'

'It's all right with me. Dave and Sara will be back soon. You can ask them then.'

She felt self-conscious drinking coffee with this strange young man. Her mind fumbled for the right things to say, and as usual came up with nothing. She had never been good at asking social questions, but Don didn't seem to mind.

'I'll have to start working soon. I make shoes, and as I'm still learning , it takes me a whole day to get a pair of sandals together. I've got two to finish before tomorrow. Come in and talk to me if you want. But I'll show you the room you can have first.'

She picked up her mug of coffee and followed him into the passage.

'This is my room,' he gestured, 'and next to it the bathroom and where we do the washing up. Opposite is the room you can have.' It was small, the width of a mattress, with that and a rose-pink carpet its only furniture.

'This is the way we get out onto the roof', said Don, opening one of the two windows. She stared out through the broad leaves of a sycamore tree at an extraordinary garden. Don had gone by then, disappearing suddenly into his own life, leaving her free to gawp at an extensive and untidy ruined regency house which seemed to have been forgotten by the rest of the world. The mews, she realised, must have been the servants' quarters and coach house to this grand place which had iron stairs leading up to balconies with large graceful windows, now gaping holes, the shutters hanging over air. Between her and the ruined house was a small patch of untended garden, where more sycamores, an elder and a cherry tree had grown up unhindered. All this devastation, if it was that, it seemed so beautiful, had been here for some time to have allowed big trees to establish themselves where once people had lived, warmed themselves, cooked, talked and slept.

The mews was on the first floor so she was looking

5

down and across at the ruin. She had no idea how large it was, but it seemed to be more than just a facade. As she stared, a large white rabbit came lumbering into view, making its way towards a pile of cabbage leaves under the elder tree.

This was enough invitation. She put down her coffee mug and clambered through the window onto the flat roof outside. There was a ladder against the wall. She was wearing jeans so she had no trouble negotiating the steps. First she greeted the rabbit, who didn't seem to mind her, but was more interested in the cabbage leaves. Then she picked her way through doorways into a maze of rooms, one leading off from another, open to the sky, their floors now earth only. There was a dampish smell of old leaves, she passed a fig tree which was growing through a crack in the wall and spilling over onto an iron balcony. Further in it seemed spooky, too quiet, as if the space no longer welcomed her, as if it forbade her entry. She passed a huge marble fireplace set into the wall fifteen feet above her head, turned a corner and came across two concrete lion's paws standing next to a pile of rubble.

The place had a chill about it even on this summer's day and wanting to return to the graceful image she had had at first, the stage set for a magical transformation scene, she had a moment of panic. Would she be able to find her way back? Her first impulse was to run, but she made herself walk back the way she had come and, indeed, there was the opening into the garden, the white rabbit, the ladder back to the safety of the mews and even though there was little sunlight because of the trees, the summer heat returned to ease her nerves.

When she climbed back through the window of her room, there was a young man sitting on her mattress. He had dark black hair and was powerfully built, although not very tall. He sat quietly, waiting for her to clamber through before he spoke: 'Jean?' It was only then that she realised that he was blind.

'Yes, that's right,' she replied.

'I'm Mark. Christopher spoke about you. He visited your home didn't he? And I met Jeremy once too, I think, when he was at Warwick for a conference.'

She sat down in front of him on the pink carpet.

'I'm glad to be here. Just been outside in the ruins. What an extraordinary place. Who is the white rabbit?'

'Oh – Cocaine – he's lived here for over a year. You'd better ask Sara about him. I think we were looking after him for someone and he just stayed. I expect he's squatting, like us.'

'Please explain that to me,' said Jean. She would have to learn what this word really meant. After the experience outside everything seemed possible. 'Would you like some coffee first?'

'I'll make it,' replied Mark, getting up. 'Do you take milk and sugar?'

Over the coffee Mark explained that Sara had been the first person to move into number five, which had been left empty by the Crown Commission, who owned all the lovely houses round the park. The Crown Commission was not exactly the Queen herself, but some board who managed the property for the benefit of – whom? Jean wasn't sure. In any event their plan seemed to be to rebuild the ruins which hadn't been touched since a bomb had dropped on them during the war, and to demolish and rebuild some of the houses round them, but to do that they needed to get all the legal tenants out and to have enough money for the building works.

So in this area there were too many empty houses, waiting indefinitely to be pulled down, and Sara, with other homeless young people, had moved in.

'I see you all have keys for the front door, though,' said Jean, still confused about how anyone could just walk into empty property and camp there without being thrown out.

'Oh yes. Once you occupy a house that's empty, you change the locks and then no one can get you out until they have a court order.'

'Wouldn't they do that straight away?'

'No. The court won't grant an eviction order unless the owners are ready to start work because there are too many speculators buying up property and making people homeless. And the speculators don't mind if the houses fall

7

down. In fact they even employ people to wreck them so that they are uninhabitable. It's a national scandal when so many people are without anywhere to live.'

'So you don't pay rent, then?'

'No, but we do pay rates to Camden Council, which are quite high because it's a posh area. As far as the Crown Commission is concerned, we don't live here, and if we paid rent we would have tenants' rights, but they must know we're paying rates, because otherwise *they* would have to . . . I suppose.'

They sat for a moment in silence. Jean had met a few blind people before, friends of her father's who had been blinded in the war, remote, jolly men with wives who shielded them from harm, read their books to them, gave them children. Mark seemed different, more independent, although more chaotic, his shirt was torn at the elbows, his socks in his sandals were obviously from different pairs. But perhaps that wasn't because he was blind, but because of who he was.

'If you want to ask more questions about squatting, I'll take you down to Chester Square. I'm going anyway, I grind the flour for the bread they make at the community shop. You can meet Walter and Janet who run it. Would you like to come?'

'Yes, please.'

Mark had a collapsible white stick which he took with him, but he taught her to give him her arm in such a way that she was imperceptibly ahead of him, giving him the signals he needed to know whether the ground went suddenly up or down. Then there would be no necessity to guide him with words.

But it was he who guided her. They made their way through a large council estate and across a busy road towards an area which was clearly very run down. They passed a battered pub surrounded by narrow victorian houses. Jean and Mark walked as closely as lovers. In spite of being strangers, they had broken through the physical distances between people. For this reason Mark's blindness made it possible for her to confide in him her most personal feelings.

Christopher had already given him the facts of her life. She told him how she felt about having to begin again. How afraid she was that she would never find anything good in life. How disappointed she had been in her marriage, and in what it had done to her, making her frightened of being herself, always glad to play second fiddle to her husband, the professor, and yet dependent on him for her self-image, which he had reflected back at her, distorted and finally rejected.

Mark allowed it all to flow over him. 'My mother feels like that,' he commented, 'but she is still trapped in it. She isn't strong enough to leave my father and he is Catholic and will never leave her. She's very beautiful. She loves him, but they have lost each other somewhere. They started off with a very passionate relationship.'

'My mother', the words gave her a sudden chill. Was this how she was being regarded by the community she was entering? It was natural for him to say it, she was old enough, but how would she escape from these labels, my mother, my wife. She was misguided to think she could relate to the world just as herself, Jean. She had wanted somewhere to stay, had been given a room, at least for a short time and in a place that was as far away from what she had left as she could have wished, yet she was still not free to decide who she was. Mark was blind, could not judge her by how she looked, and indeed she had prided herself always that she did not show her age, but that was vanity. She was who she had been, a mother, a wife. Her years of experience could not be thrown away.

In her disappointment her body stiffened involuntarily and Mark, sensing this, kept quiet the rest of the journey. She no longer looked about her with pleasure. All her life she had been dependent on the way other people saw her. When she was young, she had worried about not being beautiful enough, now she checked her make-up each time she passed a mirror, re-applied lipstick when she went out, caught horrified glimpses of herself in shop windows. How had she imagined it could be possible to make herself over again when she still relied on other people's opinions of her? Stephen had known that, his admiration of her, so often expressed during their courtship, had deteriorated into a catalogue of her faults; her stupidity, her selfishness, her inadequacy. Trapped by her own weakness, he had made her weaker, so that it was only when he had quite literally kicked her out that she had summoned the strength to say to herself that she wanted to start over.

But start over where? She had considered returning to university, where she and Stephen had first met and where she had given up her studies to carry their first child. But somehow the idea of studying didn't appeal to her now. It was too late for that doctorate in psychology and besides, she had seen too much of academic life and of the women who worked in universities, always satisfied with the less spectacular positions because they lacked the charisma of 'popular' male lecturers who could entertain eager students with their cynical wit or dominate the university bar at the end of the day.

No, it was hard to find out what she should do, and even harder when the models held out to her were none of them what she wanted, nor was what she saw in the mirror enough to reassure her. Yet she still had strength to refuse, and that she would do. She wanted no part of the university world which Stephen inhabited. She refused to be seen as a mother, she could not be satisfied with the giving love her own mother had chosen to make into a way of life. Now she was in London, in a new place with new people. They were strangers to her, younger than she was, but that was not her choice. Her own age group were not in a position to give her the freedom she wanted; so clearly labelled as they were, all they offered her was the position of a rejected wife who would make the best of a bad job, settle down quietly and hope that one day, although it was probably unlikely, a man her age, a kindly widower perhaps, would ask her to share his loneliness with him.

Mark seemed to understand her confusions. 'You know,' he said, 'I fight stereotypes too.'

She could not tell how much it cost him to say that, but she was grateful for it and was to remember it often when things went less well between them.

Chapter Two

Chester Square was clearly a squatting community. The lamp-posts were gaily painted in carnival colours. On the side of a sagging building held up by wooden buttresses was scrawled in large white letters: 'Squat now while stocks last.' Music drifted through an upstairs window. The front door of one of the houses was propped open. This was the community shop.

Mark led Jean inside and down the passage. A door opened onto two large rooms with light entering from windows at the front and at the back. Walter and Janet were busy at one end, where there were shelves with plastic bags of rice and fruit and nuts packed neatly in labelled rows. They were older than Jean had expected, perhaps her age or even older. She was immediately attracted to Walter, he had a long grey beard and spoke with that kind of male authority that she admired. Janet was so different from her, her face without make-up was serene, her long skirt trailed noiselessly on the floor through the large clean rooms where sacks of beans and peanuts and lentils stood waiting to be weighed, below shelves of honey and home-made peanut butter and warm bread.

Both Walter and Janet stopped their work to welcome them.

'This is Jean,' Mark told them. 'She's come to stay at the mews. She wants to know about squatting. Tell her about the square.'

Walter led Jean to a street map pinned up on the wall.

'This is where we are,' he said, pointing to a circular area he had outlined in red pencil. 'There are lots of squats here. In a way we form a community that is defined for us by the devastation around us. Look. Here's Euston tower and the railway line, here they've pulled down houses for a multi-storey car park, this is a main road and here' – his hand completed the circle on the map – 'is a huge complex belonging to IBM. We're all that's left.'

'Not for long,' said Mark.

'No. But if you start thinking about housing and food, you know where to start changing things. That's why we run the shop. Take meat, for example – '

'Oh no! Please don't make me give up bacon sandwiches and sausages,' pleaded Mark in mock horror.

'You can joke, but you can't start a revolution on bangers and mash.'

'I won't let you make me feel bad about my eating habits. I'm off to grind your wheat for you – and me.' And Mark tramped off downstairs to the kitchen in the basement, leaving Jean standing in the corner of the upstairs room, watching people come in for their bread or for a pound of dates or figs from boxes marked *Israel* or *Turkey*.

The room was a strange mixture of country puritanism and eastern mysticism. The wood of the doors and skirtings and indoor shutters had been carefully stripped of paint and waxed a clear golden brown. The floor boards were stripped and waxed too and there was a old grate for an open fire. It was extremely clean. On the wall above the fireplace was an embroidery of an Indian god in dark plum with little mirrors and there were several Indian cushions under the window.

When it was quiet again, Janet asked if she would like tea and they sat outside in a cement yard at the back with the teapot on a packing case with mugs and milk. ('Sugar is poison, you know,' said Janet.) Jean promised to bring herbs from her mother's garden – mint, sage, rosemary and thyme, It was so peaceful here, so easy to envy this kind of lifestyle –

the life and the work merging into one whole, no rough edges. Or were there?

'You must come to a meal,' said Walter. 'I'll cook it.'

'I'd like to –' interjected Janet.

'No. I'll do it. You can't cook.' Jean winced at the tone of his voice. She didn't want to hear it, nor did she want to see Janet's almost imperceptible flinch. She excused herself and went down the stairs to look for Mark.

'I think I'll go back now,' she said when she saw he was nowhere near finishing. 'Thank you for bringing me. I'll remember how we got here.'

On the way back to her room in a place where she was still a stranger, she bought fruit and tea and milk. She was beginning to understand that as she was not paying rent, and as Christopher had not paid rent, it was not in his power to offer her his room. She remained dependent on Sara and Dave for their permission or approval, and especially on Sara because, although the men dominated the mews, Sara was its centre. She was sure of this because of the way both Don and Mark had talked about her. It was Sara who had first changed the lock on the door, who had put down the carpet and provided the crockery and the other essentials for living there. Christopher had said that they had sat in her room at night and listened to her records before the kitchen was fixed up, that she was sleeping with Dave, who was very speedy and who had the most energy in the house. All the other people she had met that day had accepted her without questioning who she was and where she came from. She was fearful that Sara would not. Oh, she told herself, don't fuss so. You can always make a different arrangement if they tell you you can't stay.

This time when she rang the bell, there was immediately activity inside. There was a shout of: 'I'll go', and the sound of boots clattering down the stairs. The door was opened by a tall young man in a long, pale beige cotton dress. His arms were too long for the sleeves, while his legs stuck out under the skirt and ended in Dr Marten's boots.

'Hello, you're Jean,' he said and turned to go upstairs

again, while she shut the door and gathered her parcels together. 'I'm Dave,' he announced over his shoulder in a friendly voice.

'I bought some tea and some milk,' Jean replied. Damn, why, in moments of stress, did she fall back on her mother's role of food provider? 'I'll make tea,' she went on as she got into the room. 'Do you want some?'

There was a young woman sitting on the floor, drawing. This was Sara. Her reddish-brown hair fell forward over a pale, round face. She was wearing a long dress with wide sleeves which hung over her wrists and a low cut neck. She looked up and smiled, but the two women were guarded towards each other. As Jean walked over to the cupboard to put down her purchases and then to fill the kettle, Dave seemed to be everywhere. His image came between her and Sara, he twirled his long skirt, threw out his arms like a model, curved his body into its most elegant shape.

'I love this!' he exclaimed, 'Why don't we go down Oxford Street dressed up in each other's clothes? I love make-up. Women have a much better time than men.' He rushed from the room towards Sara's room and re-appeared with lipstick and eye shadow and a mirror. 'Help me, Sara. How do you do this?' Sara dropped her drawing to make up Dave's face. Jean took mugs to the bathroom to wash them. When the tea was made, Dave was ready to leave. 'Come on,' he urged Sara and Don, who was now also trying on different dresses and looked like an enchantingly innocent girl in another long dress which belonged to Sara. Sara wore a striped shirt and waistcoat with a pair of tweed trousers that were too long for her, but which she managed to shorten at the waist and keep up with a belt. She was slightly taller than Jean – with a plumpness that was still part of being in her teens. She piled up her hair under a bowler hat and put on clown make-up. Don was outlining his eyes with mascara. Everything was happening in a rush, Dave's idea pushing them all forward. They gulped down their tea and were gone, leaving Jean to dream alone in the room which was now piled with discarded clothes, spilled make-up and an even fuller ash tray.

Jean walked to her room, but it was too small and bare

to sit in and she wandered back to the main living space. She was beginning to love this house with its green light and small rooms. She wanted to caress it, cherish it, and with that in mind, she started to tidy it up. She emptied the ash tray into the large plastic bag she found near the door, collected the mugs and washed them, tidied the food on top of the cupboard, wiped down the table and the stove and the cupboard, folded the clothes, There was no broom so she went out to buy one and a small dustpan and brush, but the shops were already shut, she would have to do that the next day. Finally she watered the plant, made another cup of tea and sat down with the newspaper.

They returned sooner than she had expected them. They were delighted with themselves, had been on the escalator at Top Shop, had walked down Oxford Street through the crowds. People had genuinely taken Don for a woman, and everyone was puzzled by the three of them together. Their astonishing stories tumbled out of them:

'A man offered us parts in a film . . .'

'At the Golden Egg the waiter couldn't stop laughing . . .'

'The man selling balloons asked us to stay with him to draw the crowds . . .'

Jean, not realising how close they were to the places they spoke about, was puzzled by how quickly they could be there and back and do all that they claimed, but she was happy to smile at their success and to sit quietly while Don and Dave made a supper of vegetables and scrambled eggs, which they ate on their laps round the low table. Mark seemed to have disappeared since their visit to the square. Don put on a record.

'Do you mind the music?' he asked.

'Don't do that to me!' exclaimed Jean. 'I like it.'

'You want to stay two weeks, don't you?' said Dave.

'What would you like to hear?'' It was Don again, the question always floored her. Although she liked music, she didn't listen to it in the way that Jeremy and his friends did. She couldn't remember names and the words always seemed to be drowned by the instruments. How could she say she knew no names of songs, to people who could sing along with the words and to whom the words and music were equally important? She was afraid to lose face and mumbled:

'Oh, anything you like. Have you got Dylan?' Don was already up and soon 'Hey, Mr Tambourine Man' soothed her, calmed her fears. She was uncertain of her place here, wanted to be able to rest. She had, she realised, not done so for a very long time. It had been a long time since she had really felt at home anywhere; her mother's house had given her shelter, but when she was in it she became the daughter who asked permission to use the telephone or bring home a friend. When she was there small things irritated her. There was nowhere that was her own, there never seemed enough hot water to bathe in, and although she gardened and helped her mother clean, she did so as a duty, a chore rather than the loving care you give those objects and spaces that are dear to you. And before that, with Stephen . . . it had been a long time since she had felt that the double-storied brick house with its well-kept garden was really hers. Legally it had never been: the house and the car had always been in his name, the mortgage was in his name, even the bank account, although she had the right to sign his cheques. She was his manager though, if there were too many bills, and there often were, there were terrible rows, as if she were responsible for garage bills, book bills, electricity bills, as if she alone had spent the money wilfully. She became frightened as she recalled their monthly budget nights, her old fear returning that she could not please him. It was this same fear which made her glad now that she had refused his offer of an allowance or even a lump sum of money. She wanted nothing from him, so afraid that if she took anything she would still be accountable to him for what she did and how she spent it. She had money of her own, a small legacy from her father. It was in a separate bank account, she had taken that. It would tide her over until she could find a job.

Dave repeated his question. 'You want to stay, don't you?'

'Yes, please, if I can. Will you have me?'

Don laughed. 'Yes, I think you can stay – but only if you

buy a pair of shoes from me.'

'I'll do that anyway. Can I stay?'

She was looking at Sara, who lifted her head from her drawing. 'I've never lived with a woman before,' she said. 'Yes, you can stay.' Sara was drawing, she said, a picture of her orgasm. It was made up of flowing lines around a central burst of colour. Jean looked at it as it was passed round. She felt far less experienced than this young woman who seemed to be so in control of her own life and her body. Her own sexuality was something that had always embarrassed her. Stephen had been her only lover. When they had made love before they were married, their encounters were quick and furtive. After marriage Stephen had been less eager for lovemaking. He had disliked her telling him what pleased her. If he was to be master in his own house he didn't want his wife to tell him what to do in bed, so she had learned to be very quiet while he made love to her and to lie very still. If she did not do this it was possible that he would not make love to her at all. On the occasions when he did, he turned onto his side immediately after he had come inside her, pretending to want to sleep, leaving her awake and aroused, lying behind his broad back.

Sara's sexuality seemed so much more natural, so much her own choice, a part of her life in a way that Jean's had never been. Perhaps it went with the way she lived, Jean thought, the way she had taken the housing she needed without waiting until it was given to her. Jean felt much younger rather than older than these people who had received her so generously. She was a learner, not a teacher. She had nothing to tell them except her own confusion. Now, wanting to start all over again she felt she had come to the right place.

Yes, it felt good to be here. Dave passed round a joint. She did not know how to inhale properly, took a deep gulp of smoke and held her breath, then let it go. This was what the others had done. She felt a little wobbly-headed, but also as if she had come to rest, as if the world was gentle and kind and that everything in it, including herself, was warm and loving. Dave said that plants grew better if they were close to people who were fucking and he took the green spindly plant with him and Sara into the bedroom.

Don and Jean remained sitting. He was telling her that the previous weekend when he had gone to the latest Warhol film he had nearly been picked up by a middle-aged American tourist who asked him to come back with him to his hotel.

'Did you want to go?'

'I don't know. I can't decide things for myself, or start things, it's as if I must wait for someone else to tell me what to do.'

'Did you go?'

'No, somehow I was scared. I just said I had to get home and bicycled back here. I'm sorry really.'

There were energetic sounds from the bedroom. Jean felt like an eavesdropper, although she was curious to note that it did not seem quite as if Sara was having as good a time as she had presumed. Don and she smiled at each other in a rather embarrassed way.

'I'll do the washing up,' said Jean. 'Don't bother to help, you did the cooking.'

She gathered up the plates and the frying pan and carried them through to the bathroom. It wasn't late, but it seemed to her as if it had been a long day. She was still in a rather giddy haze, which made her each gesture slow and deliberate. Everything she did seemed to take a very long time. There was a gas heater in the bathroom so there was no problem about hot water. After I'm finished with the dishes, she thought, I'll have a bath. I can lie in the water and think about the day and what it means to be living here, even if it is only for two weeks.

Chapter Three

She was woken the next morning by Dave's face peering into hers. He was looking intently at her, his hand on her hair.

'I've brought you a cup of tea,' he said. 'Mark says you have a son who is twenty-one. How old are you?' She sat up groggily and rumpled her hair into place. Then she swallowed a mouthful of tea and thought how to answer him.

'Yes, that's right. Jeremy is twenty-one.'

'How old are you?'

'Will it make any difference how you treat me? Will it make a difference whether I can stay?'

'Of course not,' he replied and was for a moment distracted from his question. She was afraid to give him a real answer, afraid that if she said she was forty-three, they would regard it, as she did herself, as a great age. She knew she shared their prejudice against the old, thinking anyone over thirty-five past respecting. And she supposed that she had hoped that she would just be able to pass that terrible test, to look still young enough to be free, still to have choices open to her, not to be told that her life was over.

She feared that if she gave her age it would come between her and her new friends like a shutter coming down. Often she thought of herself as relating to people through the windows of a house, that she looked through two spy holes at the world. The fabric of her face seemed so solid, she could even make out the blur of her nose between her eyes. When she was tired she was aware of the face through which she spoke, could imagine the red eye-lids, the tired lines round her mouth. She tried to cover it up, improve herself, to present the kind of face she wished others to meet. She put on powder and lipstick, ran a black line round her eyes; it made her face more of a mask, but also less of a pink blob, gave her eyes a depth, rather than two pale round balls. During the day she constantly checked that face to make sure it was still intact. Yet it never satisfied her. When she spoke to someone, she looked at them. She knew they were both seeing and hearing her at the same time, the two messages being received simultaneously. She wanted to control what they saw. It was for this reason that she worked so hard on her face and on her clothes, trying to achieve the right balance between spontaneity and calculation.

When she got up, she found that she had to compete in the bathroom with all the other sleepy people in the house. Sara was lying in the bath, the water buoying up her soft breasts. Dave was brushing his teeth and Don was making toast on the grill in the kitchen. Mark had been out drinking and had returned in the early morning. He had been up since then, reading, and was just preparing for bed. 'It's quieter at night. I like to read then,' he said. 'There's more tea in the pot if you want some.' She sat down with him and poured herself another mug of tea.

When Sara came through she was wrapped in a large brown towel with her hair still wet from the bath. She sat next to Jean and asked her whether she would like to accompany her to the vegetable market at Camden Town. They could walk through the park and maybe stop in the rose garden. It was already promising to be a very warm day. Jean got ready to go out.

By the time they set off it was almost noon. It was one of those perfect summer days when the sky is complete blue and the sun bounces off the grass freeing the smell of the lawn into the still air. They walked slowly, Sara was carrying a large yellow woven bag with her purse in it. She was wearing a long Indian cotton skirt and a sleeveless cotton T-shirt. Jean wore a long backless sun dress. It was too hot for trousers. Their skirts swished against the grass as they walked.

'Did you say you were going to the conference on Saturday?' asked Sara.

'Yes. I read about it in *Spare Rib*. I've never been to one and it seemed interesting.' Jean was hesitant about feminism. Women's libbers seemed to her a little shrill. She was afraid of being called one and of being laughed at by men and by other women. It was a relief to hear that Sara also wanted to go and that she was suggesting they they went together. The conference was to be in some school building quite a distance away, but Sara semed to know how to get there. It meant changing tubes, Sara said.

'There's also the abortion march. Will you still be here for that?'

'Abortion': even the word sounded shocking. When Jeremy was a year old, Jean had become pregnant again. Stephen had planned to study that year, it was his sabbatical. If they had another child he would have to give up the scholarship he had been awarded to Chicago University. The pregnancy would have been embarrassing. Jean thought people would say they bred like rabbits. It seemed obvious to her that she must have an abortion although at that time it was difficult to know how to get one. The doctor she asked said that he had no intention of performing it. She should not have asked him, he said. In the end Stephen arranged it. He had a friend who had got a girl into trouble and had found someone to do it. His friend said it had been all right.

One morning a middle-aged woman carrying a carpet bag had come to the house. Jean had let her in. She asked for boiling water into which she mixed a large quantity of strong soap. Jean and she went into the bathroom which had a washable floor. She told Jean to squat down and inserted something sharp into her vagina and then a tube with the warm soapy solution. Jean felt a sharp pain and then the warm soapy water trickled down her legs. The woman said

21

she should lie down and called Stephen, who was waiting in the living room, to come to his wife. Quite soon afterwards Jean began to bleed. Two days later she had an overwhelming urge to go to the toilet. Something large plopped out with a lot of blood. She called Stephen because she did not want to look to see what it was. He told her, yes, it had been the child. He had looked after she had returned to bed and he had flushed it down the toilet.

That was the last time they spoke about it. She had felt ashamed and guilty for what she had done, had somehow assumed that she alone was reponsible for the death of that child, that Stephen had had nothing to do with it. Later she always lied to doctors who asked her if she had had an abortion when they filled in forms. Between her and Stephen it was as if the event had never happened, it became yet another part of their life together which was never talked about.

Yet now women were shouting the word aloud in demonstrations, writing it on posters: 'Abortion on demand'. She didn't know what she thought about that. It was as if women were smearing their menstrual blood on the streets, leaving their wounds open for all to see. 'Why is the march taking place now?' she asked.

'Well, the Act is under threat, but even with it, it's really not easy to have an abortion. A lot of doctors won't do it and when they do it on the National Health they make sure you wait weeks so that you need to have a saline drip which is very painful. Dave got someone pregnant and he paid for an abortion so that she could have it quickly. Luckily I could give him the money. I was working then, I was a sales girl at Top Shop until last month.'

'When is the march?'

'It's the Saturday, a week after the conference. You'll still be here, won't you?'

'Yes, I'll stay for that.' Already she was becoming involved with the life of the city in a way that did not happen in Winchester. Jean felt she wanted to embrace the city. They had reached the rose garden and stood together for a moment just taking it all in. There were deep red roses and silvery pink, sudden yellow and apricot. The bushes were planted in beds of colour, each making a separate statement. There were pergolas looped with sprays of single white stars. There were columns of roses, walls of roses, beds of roses, climbing roses, standard rose bushes, old roses and the latest hybrid. Each new rose was a discovery, as if nothing else in the world could be so beautiful, until the next one, which was equally perfect. They walked through them as if in a dance.

'I'll buy you tea,' said Jean pointing to a pagoda-like tea room set in a dip in the landscape.

They took trays of tea and danish pastries to a white table outside where they could still see the roses and where they had to defend their food from sparrows and over-eager pigeons. 'It's like being in that Hitchcock movie!' exclaimed Jean, and they laughed.

'Didn't you mind about Dave getting someone else pregnant and you having to pay?'

'No, I don't think so. He cares about me. He wants me to be more liberated. He has taught me so much about myself and made me love my body, which I was always so ashamed of. I thought I was too big. He says he would love to join the women's movement to help them.'

'Do you think he should be allowed to?'

'I don't know. Perhaps we shouldn't exclude really nice men.'

*   *   *

Sara looked at Jean. She thought how odd it was that she was enjoying this day so much. Usually her life was grey when Dave wasn't around, as if she only came alive when he was there. It was nice having a friend to confide in. And Jean, although she was older, seemed so eager to find out about her life that Sara felt quite experienced in her company.

Jean had short curly light brown hair which was very soft, and big green eyes. She's not pretty, thought Sara, it's a nice face, but sad though.

Jean was looking towards a man and woman at the next table. Her eye followed their every movement. She's staring, thought Sara, a little disapproving, and then noticed why.

The man was talking. He was writing a book, he was telling the woman why it was so interesting. 'Yes,' she responded, 'I see. But if you . . .' The man wasn't listening. He heard only the affirmation. He was talking again.

Jean turned her head back to Sara and smiled.

'I'm sorry. Jeremy always tells me I stare at people. I think I do it more since I've been alone. It's almost as if I'm outside and everyone else is inside somewhere. So I watch them a lot.'

Sara was amazed that Jean could know those feelings. When she was at school, Dave was the leader of the sixth form and she was his woman. They were rebels togther. She had felt strong and proud, strong enough to defy her parents and even to look down on them a little. Dave had done that, so it must be right. His parents were easy-going, tolerant of him and his exploits, which made hers seem painfully protective and nagging. But when she had come to London, Dave had been living in the square and the mews had seemed so big and empty with just her in it. She had felt alone and frightened. There had been days when she had been too frightened to go out. Jean was seeing her in a different phase, with lots of people around her and Dave had even moved there in the last week.

Now Dave wanted her to be stronger, more independent. He kept meeting other women who were taking a stand for women's rights. He wanted her to be like them and gave her books to read which she would not otherwise have bought. I can't just change overnight into what he wants me to be, she thought. She felt like a bird beating its wings against the bars of its cage. But he wasn't a cage. How could she say that? He understood what it was to be a woman and he loved her and made her love herself. Even her body seemed beautiful when he showed it to her. She remembered how he had given her a mirror, and told her to squat over it. 'Look,' he had explained, 'you can see yourself, see how you fit together.' She had been shy at first, but she had never refused him anything and when she looked, it was a marvel. She had never before really explored that rosy place with its soft, glistening folds. Yet she was still aware that he was watching her to see how she would react, so she wasn't quite able to know her own feelings.

She felt bad thinking like this. As if it meant that she didn't love Dave, and that was impossible, but she also felt safe with Jean, who didn't know much about feminism, didn't even know as much as she did, but who asked questions. Jean didn't seem to be critical of her answers, so it was almost as if she was thinking aloud. Perhaps Jean would become more her friend than Dave's.

'I think I'll buy a broom in Camden,' said Jean.

'You don't have to,' laughed Sara, 'You can stop doing housework now, you know. By the way, you don't say Camden, it's Camden Town.'

'All right then: Camden Town. But I'll still buy the broom. I want to give the mews a really good sweep. It's so lovely there.'

Chapter Four

London was experiencing the hottest June for fifty years. That was what the newspapers said. The city seemed transformed into a continental capital like Rome or Athens. It smelled of heat, the tar melted and Jean was surprised how her clothes became dirty within a few hours. The pace of life was slow, people lounged in doorways chatting, sat outside drinking beer in the strong sunlight, came home in the evening dusk, still without needing a jacket. On Saturday night they made a late night excursion to the cinema, while the Sunday evening was spent on the roof outside Jean's window, drinking cider and listening to the sound of a guitar played by the musician who lived downstairs.

Jean found that she had become part of a community of people who had squatted many of the houses in the street on the other side of the mews. There were avante garde ballet dancers, young people from France or Italy who had come to London for the summer, people who had taken up squatting as a political gesture because they were so angry at all the empty houses, or others who just needed the space to live on their own. Everyone seemed to be doing something. There were musicians and artists, there were religious people who didn't eat meat, and sometimes not even milk or eggs, who were teaching and learning yoga or meditation.

All these visited the mews, ringing the doorbell or climbing in unexpectedly through her window.

They talked to Don, who sat quietly working at his shoes, made themselves tea, gossiped about each other or made plans for their lives and for the country. Jean listened to them talk. When she visited the shop, which was open on Sundays as well, Walter said that this was a rest period, that when the autumn came everyone would be busy again, paint the walls of their rooms, find jobs, but that now was a time for finding oneself, for laughter and pleasure.

This was certainly true for Jean. She enjoyed the casual way people accepted her, was content just to sit quietly and listen. She made friends with a man who wore orange, who encouraged her to talk. His name was Sangito. Of course it wasn't his real name; he had been born again under his master, had been to India and was planning to go again in the autumn. He was small and dark with deft, gentle hands. She met him at the shop where he had been putting up shelves for Walter, and she visited him in his room which was very clean and white, where he made her tea with cinnamon and cummin seeds added to give it flavour. She liked having friends outside the mews, it gave her a sense of independence from Sara and Dave, Don and Mark. She was careful not to be too much with them, too clinging.

On Tuesday morning she went with Sara to the women's liberation workshop, where the conference was being planned and where women could go to buy books and magazines. The address was a busy street in the centre of London. They walked shyly through a street door with a board on it which said: *Women Only Welcome* in red letters on a white background. This was a squat too and was clearly not in a good state, the walls needed redecorating and there was a notice in the passage saying that the toilet was blocked. There was a big room downstairs with a carpet on the floor and lots of shelves with books and pamphlets displayed on them. When they entered there was a group of women round the two desks in the far corner who seemed to be old friends. Jean and Sara stood for a few moments in the doorway, wondering what they should do. Then Jean walked across the room to ask whether she and Sara could look around. 'Yes, of course,' one of the women replied, looking at her. 'There's coffee if you want it on the table over there. You just plug in the kettle and put three pence in the box. You can wash your cups in the basin in the toilet.' And she turned back to her friends.

Jean made coffee for her and Sara and they both browsed among the books. There seemed to be such a lot to read which she had never seen before. She recognised *Spare Rib*, but there were other journals, on cheaper paper, with names which seemed to go out of their way to be aggressive. There was one called *Shrew* and another, from America, called *Off our backs*. There were piles of papers which had been typed and then duplicated, and pamphlets which gave the impression that they had been printed cheaply and in a hurry, as if what was inside them needed to be read urgently. Jean felt confused by the amount of choice in front of her, ignorant about what to buy and what to think. *Sisterhood is Blooming* said one poster. She didn't know what that meant. *We are the women that men have warned us about* said another. She picked up poems by Robin Morgan because Sara said she liked them, a pamphlet on housework (that was something she *did* know about) and a book by Sheila Rowbotham, a name she had seen mentioned in *Spare Rib*.

When she had made her selection, she went over to the women, who were still talking together. She stood quietly, waiting for them to notice her.

'It was amazing, we spent all weekend with my parents and my mother even sent my little sister in with cups of tea for us on Sunday morning.'

'Well, that's not possible in my family, I can tell you.'

'Excuse me,' said Jean, addressing a tall woman sitting behind a typewriter, who had spoken to her earlier, 'I would like these books please.'

'Well, just add up the prices, they're all marked, and put your money in the box over there.' The woman nodded towards a wooden box, which contained quite a bit of silver and several pound notes. After Jean had added up what she owed and had given herself change she looked at a notice board above the table on which the box stood. There were notices about rooms: 'Please does anyone know of a room in North London in a communal house, I would also like to bring my cat.' Another said: 'Honda motor bike for sale, very cheap, good condition. I'm going abroad for a while and need the money.' In the centre was a large sheet of paper with big writing which said: 'Planning meeting for the conference. We need to sort out what workshops women want. Please come. Thursday at eight. All women welcome.'

'I think I'll go to that,' said Jean, when Sara joined her, gesturing to the notice. 'It might be interesting. Will you come?'

'I don't know. I'll tell you nearer the time.'

When they got back to the mews, Jean sat in the sun on the roof and read the poems. Sara had said they were important, written from inside the women's movement. She read: 'I want a woman's revolution like a lover.' She walked in the maze, Sara's name for the ruins, with the lines runing through her head.

'Just once in my only lifetime to dance
all alone and bare on a high cliff under cypress trees
with no fear of where I place my feet.'

The cadence of the words excited her. When the poems were violent, she felt guilty just reading them. It was impossible that she could be so angry, that she would sing about her sex in terms as violent as this woman in her 'underground' poems. But she did not say this. Her reading was like a secret vice, done guiltily.

Sara had a friend called Monica. In the early evening the three women sat in Sara's room talking over mugs of tea. Monica had been married, but was now divorced. She had a child of six who came into the room sometimes to ask for an apple or a bit of attention, but mostly he played outside with Cocaine. Monica talked about her marriage. Her husband had disgusted her because of his drinking. When he came home late at night from the pub, she would pretend to be asleep in order to avoid his embrace. She stayed at home to look after their son, had no social life of her own, but his beery breath and heavy body claimed her late at night. She spoke about it with a shudder.

Jean sat very quiet listening to her. Stephen would have been angry if she had discussed their sexual life with anyone and she had never dared do so. In any case she had not been the one to reject his advances. She remembered taking the Pill each morning because he had insisted that he didn't wish to use anything. Yet he sometimes didn't touch her for months. Perhaps she was the only one, she thought, almost envying Monica the right to say that she had been the object of such attention. She felt uneasy with such confidences, Stephen's shadow still fell on her. She excused herself and went back to her reading.

Everything she was hearing, everything she was reading excited her. It was as if all the taboos were being broken at once. Most of what she had bought was hard work getting through. The next day she sat again on the roof, the lazy heat making her yawn. That night she discussed what she was reading with Mark.

'Why do only women do housework?' she asked him.

'That's not true,' he replied. 'Maybe you just have higher standards. We all muck in here, although I know we didn't buy a broom until you came. But Sara was here too.'

'No, I don't mean that. I was thinking about myself. How I bought the food and looked after Jeremy and did the cooking and cleaning. Stephen just had his job. When Jeremy was small he'd help me out sometimes, but I still washed the nappies. And when I worked it wasn't really a job, just a way to get some extra money. That's why it's so hard to find out what I want to do now.'

It was amazing to her how often what she read or what she discussed came back to *her*. Her life, her needs. But this time it sounded different, not just her complaining. It was possible to talk about herself in this context without feeling she was taking up too much space. She knew she was letting time slip by, but she was enjoying the leisurely way she was living, late breakfasts over the newspaper and endless cups of coffee, walks in the park, discussions about marriage with Don. It was easier now when he talked about his mother to bear it when he said: 'I wish she could meet you. I think she would get a shock. But it would be good for her.'

She disliked being considered an eccentric, and did not see how this could be, but was grateful to be accepted. Yet every now and then she knew she was not like the other people in the mews. On Monday evening Don had been picked up by an older woman. He was excited by this. He talked about how he had spent all his savings in one night, mostly on taxis. All his hard work had ended in this frantic splurge. He said: 'I think she had a child once. Or an abortion.'

'How can you tell?'

'She's got a mummy tummy. Women who've had children have that. You have.'

Jean had got used to not having any privacy in the bathroom. There were too many people using it to keep it to oneself. It was easy though, because no one stared or made you feel it was anything special to be without clothes. In fact washing and bathing and the nakedness that meant was surprisingly unsexual. People's bodies were part of them, not objects separated from them to be assessed on some physical level. Actually quite a lot of the time people rushed into the bathroom on the way out or just to get water for the kettle so there was no point in ogling whoever was there too. What was surprising to Jean was that five people lived so equably in this small space, sharing this one bathroom which was also the only place which had hot and cold water and a basin to wash up in.

If she wanted privacy she could find it in her room. No one disturbed her there for long. If people visited whom she did not know, or when she wanted to read or think she could close her door and be sure that she would not be disturbed. Sometimes Mark came to talk to her in her room after he had come in from the pub. She seldom saw him in the day time. It was almost as if he was avoiding the other people in the house by turning his day upside down. The light meant nothing to him. In any event he was often at his most talkative after midnight, and she found him sitting on her bed when she came back tired after the meeting on the Thursday night.

Jean still felt that she was inhabiting two worlds and

this made her uneasy. There were to be workshops on marriage, on pornography, on women and the law, women and social security. It was still odd for her to think of herself as belonging to an exclusive group, she still found the idea of *Women Only* notices uncomfortable. She did not say so to the women she met, they seemed so sure that they knew the way they were going and she had no clear idea where she was. It was to Mark that she voiced her doubts.

'I know we have to struggle as women, separately, until we have achieved the revolution. But it won't be forever. When we are equal we'll be able to come together again, don't you think?'

Mark was in touch with a radical organisation of disabled people. It was the only one, so he wrote for it even though he said it wasn't radical enough. He believed that a new society would not value people simply in terms of how much they could earn. The world, he said, was run for sighted and able-bodied people and only occasionally were ramps put up outside public buildings for wheel chairs. The tubes still had steps. He went all over London on his own and Jean, who was only beginning to get a sense of where she was, marvelled at his courage. Yet one evening he had come in very shaken. Workmen had neglected to barricade a hole they had dug in the entrance to the mews and he had almost fallen in. He was looking for a job, but was finding it difficult to fulfil the demands that employers made. They weren't ready to make concessions or changes in their systems of filing or running an office.

'Perhaps I'll train to be an osteopath,' he said. 'I'll write away for the application forms tomorrow. They use blind people.'

Dave was the person Jean saw the least. He was much involved in the political organisation he belonged to. He would rush out in the mornings to print leaflets or return very late at night having spent the evening flyposting. At such times he made no attempt to be quiet, clumping through the house to make himself a cup of coffee, calling to Sara to ask if she wanted one.

Sometimes he talked to the two women about what he was doing. He would sprawl on Sara's bed, keeping them both in his warmth. He talked about the other women he was meeting as if they were trophies: 'Doreen says she's going to lend me her car when she goes to Ireland. I think she likes me. She's amazing, yesterday I spent four hours talking to her about feminism.'

When he left a room it looked as if a whirlwind had struck it. There would be empty packets of cigarettes, cups of coffee, a full ashtray, papers littered all over the floor. Sara did not seem to mind. It was as if she lived through him, her life quietly waiting at the mews while he went out and then came back to her with news from the battlefield. Like a mediaeval knight and his lady, thought Jean. But at the same time, in the quiet intervals when he was gone, the two women were picking their way delicately towards each other. Jean felt most relaxed with and most accepted by Sara, and Sara too was reading voraciously the same books as she was. They shared the same excitement at the new ideas they were learning about.

But Sara was often ill. She seemed to suffer from a kind of weakness which would come over her at a moment's notice. Sometimes it was asthma, other times it was just a weariness which Sara said was the residue of glandular fever that she had had as a teenager. It meant that Jean had gone alone to the planning meeting for the conference.

When she entered the room eight women were already there. They were drinking from cans of beer and seemed to know each other well. One woman had brought a bouquet of flowers from her parents' home. They were fresh garden blooms; roses, calendula and columbine. They reminded Jean of her mother's garden. She wondered how her mother would like all these new women she was meeting. They were so different from any of the women she had known before. They wore no make-up, their hair was cut short and their breasts showed full and round in the T-shirts they wore with their jeans. She felt silly with the amount of make-up she had on. Her face felt stiff under it, she wanted to find out if she looked like a clown to them, but when she went to the toilet to see, there was no mirror to check up on.

But they seemed to accept her. The woman who had brought the flowers told her in a weary, elegant voice that she had just been home for a few days, that she had sewn a woman's sign on her jeans at the knee in order to let her parents know that she was now a feminist.

'Look,' she said, crossing her leg, 'you really can't miss it, can you?' She had waited and waited for some reaction from her parents, but there had not been a tremor of recognition. She had tensed herself throughout the visit for this confrontation, but it hadn't come.

Jean said nothing during the discussion about the conference. This group had been planning it for a long time and were only finalising arrangements and decisions and making sure that everything had been done. Nor did she volunteer for any jobs to do with running the conference. She felt selfish about that, but she didn't want to get lost behind a pile of dishes. She wanted to experience her first encounter with a women's conference without any feelings of responsibility towards others.

Afterwards they walked to the pub on the corner for a drink. Jean felt very brave sitting with this group of women who talked loudly to each other, despite the stares from other people who seemed affronted at nine women drinking together without men. Wanting to save money, she ordered half a pint of lager. A man sitting near the bar with his girlfriend overheard her. 'Isn't it disgusting, look what they drink!' he said loudly. She didn't care, she felt invulnerable. She took her drink to the table where the others were already sitting down and they made a space for her.

She waited for the weekend. She hoped Sara would go with her, but she knew she would go alone if she had to. She needed this experience. All the events of the week had led up to it: the two visits to the workshop, her reading and talking. This, above all, was why she had come to London.

Chapter Five

When Jean was a child an uncle and aunt had given her a kaleidoscope for Christmas. She remembered it still; it was a cylindrical tube, when she held it to her eye, patterns of colour filled her vision and she could change the pattern by moving the wheel at the end of the cylinder nearest to her. When she did that, what looked like pieces of stained glass moved slowly, forming elaborate snow crystals or brightly coloured dancing shapes. The pattern was never repeated. She stared for hours through the cylindrical box at this wonder world which was quite self-sufficient and needed no part of the ordinary, common-sense world to sustain it.

The weekend, when it came, was like that. Only this time the colours and shapes were alive, were hundreds of women, moving, walking, talking, eating and dancing without the scrutiny of men. When she thought about it afterwards she remembered feeling bored, feeling lost, feeling lonely, but most of all the colours claimed her. She could not stop looking at the women, she was amazed at how they moved, how beautiful they were.

On the Saturday morning after registration, she and Sara went to a drama workshop. After about ten minutes of strenuous exercises, the group of ten women decided to work on a short play which could be used later as street theatre. They dressed one woman as a man, tied her up with strong ropes and brought her into the centre of the room. Each woman shouted an accusation.

'You exploit us,' shouted Jean

'You divide us,' shouted Sara.

Although she had read all that week about the need for women's liberation, Sara's phrase went through Jean like a bolt of lightning. She had always lived in a world full of men. At home there had been Stephen and Jeremy. All her women friends were merely the wives of Stephen's friends. That was why she had felt so lonely when Stephen and she had split up. Everyone else was still married. Naturally the women went the way the men did, and *they* stayed on Stephen's side. They worked with him.

Even at the mews she and Sara were outnumbered by the men. When Dave came home, no matter what they had been talking about, he claimed Sara's attention. And her own. The women naturally switched from being with each other to being with a man.

But that wasn't quite the way she thought about it when it happened. At the time the remark went through her as if it were a sword. Yes, she thought, yes. As they left the hall at the end of the workshop, Sara and Jean came together briefly.

'Why did you say that?' asked Jean. 'It was amazing, it seemed to change the way I saw a whole lot of things.'

'I don't know. I didn't really think I was going to say it. Perhaps I read it.' And then the other events of the day claimed their attention. Jean was left on her own. Sara joined up with friends. They had chosen separate workshops for the afternoon. There were queues for food, women sold Jean food tickets and dished up mountains of salads and cheese and brown bread and fruit. Everyone around Jean seemed to be arguing, discussing, enjoying being together.

Jean suddenly felt as if she had nothing interesting to say to anyone. She wandered through the building unable to make up her mind what to do next. She visited the bookshop, and then finally the bar. In the smoky haze, women were sitting listening quietly to a group of four singers who accompanied themselves on guitars and flute. The songs were clear and simple. They sang about the everyday lives of women, about the pain of those lives, the drudgery, the violence. The silence showed how much what they were singing about touched their audience. Women sat with their beer glasses held for a moment still in their hands. During a break, Jean spoke briefly to a woman in the easy chair next to her. She was an American who lived in Paris. The women's liberation movement was different there, she said, more fashionable than in Britain, wealthier.

But Jean did not know how to receive this information. What did she know about the movement? When the performers left, taped music was switched on. A middle-aged woman sitting on the small platform in the front of the room got up and began to dance. She was very drunk, had difficulty keeping steady on her feet, but she danced with her eyes shut, as if in a trance. No one stopped her even when it looked as if she might bump into one of the big speakers belonging to the sound system.

Jean felt no kinship with this woman and her ravaged face, or rather she didn't feel they should be friends just because they were the same age. She tried to evade that idea, hoping again that her age would not show, hoping to be accepted by the mass of younger women as one of them, not an older woman. Yet she envied this woman her abandon. She did not seem to mind that her lined face and sagging body were not beautiful: she danced to the music, swayed with it, her eyes shut in ecstasy. She did not seem to care that she was observed, that there was a large roomful of women sitting talking or listening to the music, smoking and drinking and perhaps looking up to see her dance in front of them.

Later that evening Jean danced too. This time in a darkened room filled with shadowy figures. It was a long time since she had danced. She felt her bones become looser, her body respond to the music. She watched the women around her and imitated their movements, wishing that *her* body would look as elegant as theirs. She was not yet part of them all, held herself a little back, but she was glad to be there. She danced alone or in a group, having found Sara and her friends, singing along with the others with a naughty smile: 'Voulez vous couchez avec moi, ce soir?' or the more stirring, 'Get up, stand up, stand up for your rights.'

On a visit to the toilet, she looked at her face in the mirror. It was flushed and happy. Her nose was shiny, her lipstick gone, her eye make-up smeared. She wiped her eyes with a tissue. She didn't need it now; no one was asking her to present a face to them. She danced alone, for herself alone. Her body responded to her will.

The next day she put on less make-up. She had been embarrassed by her painted face. When she had looked at the other women their faces seemed eager, their bodies relaxed, but most of all they seemed to belong to themselves. Perhaps they were all as frightened as she was, wanting to be accepted and afraid to ask, but they looked calmer, more able to accept who they were. They had given up, she thought, trying to be someone else.

She was ready and waiting before Sara woke up. There was another day ahead. But Sara was ill. She felt too exhausted to go with Jean, she said. So this time Jean went alone.

Although she was late, hardly anyone was about. The previous night had been a long one and women were sleeping in. Those who had turned up looked tired and crumpled. Women had travelled all through the night to be at the conference; the next day they had slept on floors in strange houses or stayed up half the night talking. The morning workshop on 'Women in a male culture' was bitter, less affirmative than the previous day.

'I'm paid to make my boss succeed,' said one woman in amazement. 'I'm just coping with that thought and it has made me so angry. There are five of us women in the office and that's all we do. And he gets the promotion.'

'I can't stand it that I'm supposed to be permanently available to any man who looks at me. They shout at me in the street, pick me up in bars, follow me.' This time a young woman with a tiny, bony body was speaking. She shuddered 'I hide in shops on my way home from work and they, he, this man is waiting for me when I come out. I hate it.'

'Whenever I see pictures of women advertising cars or stockings, I feel inferior. I don't have a body like that. I can't afford clothes like that. I try to be like them and I can't.'

'Have you seen the way they pay women to drape themselves over cars at Earls Court? It's as if our bodies are just one of the perks that go with the cars.'

'Yes. We should recognise that and work out a strategy to cope with it. We must, in order to survive.' This time it was a woman with an American accent, dressed in black.

'The only way we can define ourselves is to withdraw from society altogether.'

'But that means loneliness, isolation.'

'So? What's new?'

There was a pause. Everyone looked down at the floor or out of the windows. Jean looked at the faces to see if she could find anyone who would give them hope. She was aware that the two previous speakers knew each other, it was apparent in the way they argued together. Now another woman joined in. She wore a loose flowery blouse over her jeans and spoke more gently than the other two.

'We could have each other, support each other. Wouldn't that be enough?'

'It doesn't work like that. You know better than that.'

Jean sat silent, listening. She felt unable to speak, her emotions were still dark inside her. She heard a woman say: 'It's war. It's total war.'

'Science, technology will be used against us if we rebel. I'm not lying. It will be, unless we can first learn how to use it.'

'*And* control it.'

They were sitting in a room which was obviously a classroom. There were no curtains on the big, high windows and the chairs were wooden with straight backs. Altogether. they were twelve women, at least half of whom were smoking. There were no ashtrays. Some paper cups with yesterday's coffee in them also contained cigarette stubs in damp heaps. One woman had found the tin rubbish bin to use as an ashtray. The room smelled stale from yesterday's cigarettes and the air was full of smoke.

The door banged open as a woman entered carrying an open can of beer. She made no attempt to close the door but let it bang shut behind her as she walked across the room, her feet loud on the wooden floor. She did not join the circle, but sat on a desk near the window. Her arrival interrupted the discussion. In spite of the discomfort of their surroundings, the members of the group had just begun to trust each other, they were thinking aloud, their ideas moving forward hesitantly, like a set of cards balanced delicately one on top of the other. Now the card house was in danger of being toppled. Jean held her breath.

'Whaddya talking about?'

No one replied for a moment, then the woman in black spoke.

'The workshop is called "Women in a male culture".'

'Culture? Come on. I don't understand what you're saying. How do you expect most women to understand what you're saying when you use such big words. You make it impossible for me to be in the movement, and people like me. You and your fucking elitist talk.'

'We were saying,' the woman explained further, 'that we have to turn away from men in order to survive. And that if we do that we will need each other.' She turned to the others. 'I think we should discuss the possibility of direct action. Something to make sexism visible. Like destroying porn magazines.'

'Naa. We've tried that. We did it in '72, don't you remember?' The woman wagged her finger at them, hectoring them. 'Useless. Doesn't work. Got caught. Not possible.'

A young, eager woman, perhaps a student, leaned forward. She was asking to be told what had happened in '72, but the account was rambling and didn't seem to fit with what they had been talking about. It was nearly time for lunch. First one woman got up to leave, then another, until there were only two or three people left in the room. They had not been able to challenge this woman, and had preferred to escape from her and from a possible confrontation with her.

It isn't so simple, thought Jean. Men divide us, use up all

our energy, but that's not all of it. We hurt each other. We can't be different just because we want to be.

The afternoon meeting was a general one in the main school hall. About a thousand women sat together, some on the chairs placed in rows across the width of the room, others on the tables pushed against the wall. Although Jean could not follow all the arguments, there seemed no end to the violence of the divisions between the women who argued and screamed and cried through the microphones placed on the floor at the platform end of the hall. Perhaps, she thought, this is all it will ever be, just the anger and pain, nothing more. Perhaps there's no room for anything else.

When she returned to the mews, Sara and Dave were out. Mark was sitting reading and she made them some tea and joined him. He'll help me not to feel like this, she thought. I don't want to be anti-men.

'I'm so afraid,' she said hesitantly, 'that if men won't change we'll learn to do without them. Leave them out.'

'What do you mean?'

'Well, why aren't men angry too? I'm white and I'm angry about racism. I stop to argue or fight if anyone is racist. Why don't men feel like that about sexism?'

'Maybe they just don't see it as a priority. Maybe everyone only has a limited amount of energy and you can't take issue about everything.'

'But we *are* a priority. We're half the population.' Jean's words cut into the air between them. She felt her body harden. 'If men don't change we'll just separate altogether. We don't need this oppression. We could do without it. We can do without men.'

'You couldn't. Women couldn't live without men.'

'Why not? We don't need so many men to reproduce. And orgasms we can give ourselves or each other, better probably. What do we get out of being with men?'

'But you couldn't run anything. You wouldn't know how. You wouldn't be able to.'

It was in the open now; she saw it for the first time. Not just in her past, finding out about her life with Stephen, or in general statements made about 'women's oppression', but here, in this room, as it happened, with someone she had trusted, she saw it.

There was nothing to say. She lay on her bed until it was time to go to sleep, then she brushed her teeth and took off her clothes. She lay in the darkness for a long time before she fell asleep. She felt entirely alone.

Chapter Six

Monday morning was cold and cloudy. A depression had moved in from the west and enveloped the island. No one sat out in the park, except in the warmest corners sheltered from the wind. The climate in the mews changed too. After Sunday's conversation, Jean felt out of tune with Mark, who now seemed to sleep all day and woke only at night, leaving marmite and marmalade on the bread knife as evidence of his midnight lifestyle, butter smears on the bread board. He was clearly depressed because he was unable to find work. Sara continued to be ill, and the street theatre she and Jean had planned to do togeher was cancelled.

And Dave – there was Jean's greatest trial. He and Don were not getting on together: they had set up some kind of competition about who was politically more correct. Dave rushed in and out with posters and pamphlets, exclaiming over cups of coffee he left for others to tidy that everyone knew that Gordon was a 'trot' or that everyone knew that the new left wing bookshop which had started in the square was libertarian and therefore suspect. He was bursting out of Sara's room and needed a place to work, he said. There was an article he had promised to write which was already overdue. He knew, he said, that Jean had not realised that she was occupying his room, or the room which was to be his, and that she would be gone soon, but all the same, he had problems about where to put his stuff and he should have somewhere to work. He had been living in the square and the people there wanted to use the room in the basement which he had occupied. He brought in a box of books and stored them in a corner of Jean's room. He borrowed Sara's sewing machine and put up curtains at the windows. 'I hope you don't mind,' he said, 'I'm giving you some curtains.' He brought in a refrigerator from the house next door, carrying it triumphantly up the stairs saying: 'Look, someone gave me this.' Jean, who was becoming more discriminating about the people in the house, wondered cynically whether this was supposed to be further proof of his lovableness.

Don grumbled over the sandals he was making. Noticing the collection of debris on his carpet which lay scattered in a circle round the spot where Dave had just been sitting, he pointed with his finger at each separate item, moving it with each different word. 'This,' he remarked bitterly, pointing to a crumpled cigarette packet, 'is an example of man's', pointing to a dirty ashtray, 'inhumanity', pointing to an empty coffee cup, 'to man', pointing to a crumpled newspaper.

Jean brought cups of tea and the newspaper to where Sara lay in her bed. On one of these occasions she expressed some of her irritation about Dave.

'He never asks whether *we* do anything. He just assumes we have no political experience at all. I mean, I was in the CND for years until I got arrested and then Stephen said I must think what would happen to Jeremy, so I stopped.'

'You should tell him.'

'No. Why should I have to? It's not the way to talk about struggle.'

On Wednesday morning it was warmer and Jean escaped to Sangito. As she stood ringing his doorbell, he came towards her across the square. He was smiling, his arms open in a gesture of welcome. It was so marvellous to be received thus that she ran towards him and into his embrace.

'I'm on my way to buy a polaroid camera for India. There's a shop at Euston Station. My father sent me the money. Do you want to come?'

'Oh, yes,' she replied and they walked arm in arm through the streets. In the shop, the assistant showed Sangito how the camera worked and took a test snapshot of them together outside under the awning. Sangito gave it to her, the two tiny figures smiling into the sunlight. Sangito was small, almost as short as she was, with curly black hair and a narrow face. They looked nice together, she thought.

On the way back to his room she confided in him.

'I don't know where the politics will take me. I feel so unable to scream and shout at people. It's not like me.'

And he hugged her and said: 'I like you as you are.'

In his room they sat close together, drinking his fragrant tea. She could feel the hairs on his arm touch her own, they were so close, yet still apart. She liked his arms: they were thin, but sturdy, his veins and muscles standing out under the skin on the soft inside arm. She put her hand on his and he set down his tea and turned to kiss her.

He pulled her shirt out of her skirt and stroked her back, her breasts. She unbuttoned his shirt so that she could feel his breast against hers. She trusted him. She wanted to feel all of him and took off her clothes while he undid his belt and slid off his jeans. He held her briefly in his arms, his body cool against hers and then put his mouth to her cunt. She felt his tongue, soft and moist, caress her. She had never felt such pleasure, it was like gentle ice skating on her body. The pain was exquisite. She held his curly dark head between her legs. Her body moved against his mouth and she came quickly in great shudders. They made love all afternoon. A warm breeze came in through the open windows, the hum of the city far below them. He stroked her body, his penis came soft and insistent inside her. Everything he did was so different from the way she had been living for the past years that she couldn't believe it was happening to her, to the Jean who had arrived in London such a short time ago and who now belonged, at least for the moment, to a whole new community of people, even her body warmed and used in ways she had never before experienced.

When she returned to the mews, Sara was up and reading on the roof.

'Oh, I'm so glad you're better,' said Jean and came to sit with her. She did not tell Sara about Sangito, nor did she speak much about Dave. With all these silences between them, they were still awkward together, yet they were busy establishing a friendship.

'I think I *will* stay for the abortion demo on Saturday. It's all happened so fast, I can hardly believe it is nearly time for me to think of leaving again. Will you be going with anyone else?'

Sara had a whole group of women with whom she had shared such experiences before. A school-friend was coming down from Leeds for the demonstration, and she would probably also be staying at the mews.

'Will it be very big?'

'Yes. Some trades unions support it. And the students union. There should be thousands.'

They drifted into a decision to go to the pictures. The warm air was blowing back over London, people were again sitting out on the pavements drinking beer and talking into the dusk. They covered their shoulders with shawls and walked towards the West End.

'We'll make the eight o'clock show, surely,' said Sara and they did, with time to spare allowing them to perch on a window ledge while they waited for the box office to open. Something about the two women, their relaxed pleasure in each other's company perhaps, made a passing tourist click his camera at them. Jean and Sara laughed togeher at the luxury of such a gesture.

'Do you remember the time we were photographed as one of the city sights?' Jean would ask Sara much later, but still with wonder.

They walked home through the darkened city, their shoes on the pavement the only sound among the deserted office blocks and closed pubs and restaurants. Outside the perimeter of Leicester Square and the sleazy Soho streets,

London went to bed as the pubs closed and the small Fitzrovia shops and offices were silent. Except for the parked cars, on such a night the narrow streets could belong to any century.

'It's so romantic at night,' said Jean. 'I want to take it all in and hold it close to me.'

'Yes. It's so quiet, it seems to be here just for us.'

Later they sat on the roof under a branch of the sycamore tree waiting for the kettle to boil, still enchanted by the night, not speaking very much, just an occasional sentence.

'I have some poems that I'd like you to read,' said Sara, and Jean felt overwhelmed at the gift.

'I've been writing too – how extraordinary, or rather I suppose it isn't really. It's hard not to – here – and I feel I have to write down my life somehow.'

'I worry about my age,' said Sara slowly, looking down into her lap. 'People say: "You're so young", my parents say I'm going through a phase, and all the time I'm me, now. When I first came here, before Mark moved in, I lived entirely alone in the mews. I was so scared. I was even afraid to go out, I could easily have killed myself, I was so empty.'

'Didn't you know Dave then?'

'Yes, but he was busy somewhere else. We'd been together at school. I met him when I was doing A levels, and my whole life changed, but I wanted to be strong on my own too. After the exams I went to France to work all that summer, but he came to fetch me back. I thought that when we got back to England everything would be perfect, and then, suddenly, I was alone.'

'Do you sleep with anyone else?'

'I did, but not any more. I just don't want to, now.'

'He does?'

'Oh yes, of course.'

When Sara walked she put her head forward shyly, keeping her body a little in reserve. Her round soft breasts hung loose and free inside her dresses and all men thought they were an invitation. They shouted at her on the street. She had no way of dealing with those calls of: 'Let's fuck, love', but would walk faster and scream at anyone who approached. 'Fuck off,' she would shout, 'leave me alone, pig.' And her sudden rage would spark off anger and threats from the men who had accosted her. Jean, who always walked as close to the walls as possible when she was alone and who neither saw nor heard the people she passed, admired her courage when Sara had told her. Just as she admired Sara's sexual life, the kind of freedom she accepted as her own which was a generation removed from how Jean had kept her own fragile virginity, admittedly only technically, for such had been the way of the heavy petting of that time, for Stephen, her lawful husband. And even then, she was now realising, her sexuality had been hidden from him and from herself.

She wanted to say: 'I worry about my age too', but lacked the confidence. She wanted to say: 'I like you', but feared to impose herself. She did not even consider that Dave could not love Sara and know her for what she was. It seemed to her self-evident.

'But he loves you,' she said, 'you're the one who's important to him.'

There was a sudden rush of tears to Sara's eyes. She put down her cup to take out a tissue from her sleeve and blew her nose briefly. Jean didn't understand this reaction to her remark, but she was afraid of tears and went on quickly.

'You can see it in the way he talks to you most of all. And the way he always comes back to you.'

Sara was still silent. She looked at Jean with such a wealth of unspoken gratitude that Jean was surprised. She felt awkward and tried to get Sara to speak.

'How long have you been together?'

'Two years – off and on. He does need me, I suppose. He's comfortable with me.'

'Of course. Two years means something.'

'Yes, it must, I suppose.'

Jean wondered if Sara were convinced. She looked across at the ruins. The moonlight made them seem even more insubstantial than usual. Sara broke the silence.

'I want you to live in London,' she said suddenly. 'You could apply for one of those youth and community jobs. They're always being advertised and as you're a qualified teacher you can get a good hourly rate for part-time work.'

'How do you mean?'

'Well, like in youth clubs. They're part-time sessions, mostly at night, and that would leave you free to do other things during the day. You could get involved in the National Abortion Campaign, or something like that. I spent a week last month addressing letters for them. They can use the help.'

It felt wonderful to Jean that someone wanted her to come to London. It was as if Sara was helping her to cross a stream and holding out a hand to guide her to a more secure footing.

'Where can I find out about them?'

'In *Time Out*. It's due out tomorrow. There are always loads in the classified section.'

'It's such a relief to plan something. I've been letting things drift, partly because so much else has been happening, but also because I didn't know where to start.'

It was time to move inside. They gathered up the coffee mugs and ash tray and climbed in through Jean's window. Her room was beginning to look a sorry sight. Her clothes hung behind the door or were folded near the mattress, but the space that she had found so precious was slowly being eroded. There were now a table lamp, two boxes of books, a trunk and a pile of Dave's clothes. The sewing machine was still there, ever since the time the curtains had been put up. Jean had pinned *Sisterhood is Blooming* to the wall, but the room was such a clutter that it looked out of place. Jean, who had over the years cultivated a way of walking lightly, almost invisibly on the earth because of Stephen's habit of counting her as the least important of all his possessions, felt still able to remain in the room because she knew she would be gone so soon. It did not occur to her that three nights would be a long time for Dave to wait.

But it was too long. On Thursday Dave brought in a large, high table which was exactly as long as the shorter of the two walls, as well as his typewriter. 'I'm going to build myself a desk,' he said. 'I'll get the wood from Dennis when I go over there tonight to do the duplicating.'

Jean stored all Dave's things under the table. In this

way, she thought, she could still make some sense of the space left to her. She went out and bought writing materials and wrote off for application forms for the jobs she chose. The table was useful to her, she decided, spreading herself over its surface, puzzling out what to include in each letter.

But on Friday everything changed. Dave brought in wood and tools during the night and started work early in the morning, impatient to get going. Dumping a record player and speakers on her bed, he said: 'I'm sorry to wake you, but I must get started. I want the desk to be finished today so that I can work tonight. They need the article by tomorrow and I'll have to work through the night. Do you think you could sleep in the kitchen?'

Jean dressed and made coffee which she drank outside. It was pleasant to be up so early. The air was still light blue, fresh-smelling; the musician downstairs was practising on his guitar. It was impossible to feel angry or even threatened. She must make plans. She didn't want to sleep on the floor in the kitchen. Somehow, she felt that it would put her in the position of a victim, the kind of position that Stephen had left her in. She did not want to feel sorry for herself. She wanted to keep her pleasure in this new place and in her new self. She did not want to feel unwelcome.

Sara climbed through the window. The sun made a halo round her head as she bent down to get through. She was carrying a cup of coffee and sat on the parapet looking at Jean.

'I want to say that I think what is happening is wrong,' she said.

'I don't want to talk about it. I know you love him. But you mustn't worry, I'm not unhappy.'

They sat in silence. Jean was thinking that she would walk over to Sangito to ask him if she could stay there for the last two nights of her visit to London. She did not yet wish to return to Winchester. She wanted to walk in the abortion demonstration. She was shy to tell Sara what she was thinking; she would have to tell her about her sexual life with Sangito and she did not want to do that.

'I'll be out for a while, but I'll be back. I've got to post those letters too.'

When Jean rang Sangito's bell, he dropped the key out of the window and called for her to come up. He had friends round. They were all dressed like him, in orange. Jean felt her blue dress looked strange in such company. She spoke to him briefly, away from the others who were planning a conference which was to take place soon.

'I can't explain now, but would it be all right if I stayed tonight and tomorrow? Is there a room in the house I could use? I must leave the mews today.'

It was all right. He would be out that day and that evening, but he would give her the key. She could come in and make herself at home, he said.

'What will you do today?' he asked.

'I'll go to the park. I have so little time left, I want to sit in the sun and read and sleep. I'll lie among the roses.'

'Sounds marvellous. I wish I could be with you.'

She returned to the mews from the park when the shadows caught up with her where she lay with her head cradled in her arms on the grass. She picked up her book and walked slowly towards the gate. She wanted to remember each moment now; the days were so few that she would be here, and London too had only a brief summer, which did not even happen every year. This was a special time, not only for her, but for all the people who walked smiling through the park or paused to feed a squirrel or watch a duck skid onto the water.

She packed her clothes into her case and her books into a plastic bag and went to say goodbye to Don. Dave and Sara were out and Mark was asleep in his room.

'You can sleep on my floor if you like,' said Don. 'You could bring your mattress in here. I think what's happened is terrible.'

'It's all right. I'm fixed up for tonight and tomorrow. Thanks anyway. I'll be seeing you.'

They hugged and then Jean carried her suitcase down the stairs and into the street. It was already dusk and the lights of the pub across the road spread yellow across the pavement. She passed people sitting like shadows at the tables outside and talking quietly over large glasses of beer. It was not far to carry the case, but far enough and she was glad to put it down as she fumbled in her bag for the key to Sangito's house. The house was deserted and quite still as she climbed the stairs to the room at the top where he lived. It was clean and empty, the two windows looked out on the square. She put down her case and leaned out of the window. She felt very alone, there was no one in the square and no one in the house. She could have been in any city: the square, in the yellow light of the street lamps looked like any slum in any country, the houses had been neglected by their owners, while the squatters and the few tenants who still lived there had given up trying to repair the crumbling facades.

She wondered what Stephen would say if he could see her now. This was a long way from the comfortable university world he inhabited. For the first time since coming to London she felt frightened. She was in a strange house in a strange part of town waiting for a man to return whom she hardly knew.

She wanted to see him, though. The memory of their lovemaking excited her. She switched on the lights and sat down on the mattress with a book, but it was impossible to concentrate. The time seemed to drag on so slowly. She could hear clocks chiming each half hour, but he did not come home. At twelve she undressed and got into bed. She lay there, waiting, the emptiness entering her, until she fell asleep. She did not hear him return and he slid into bed beside her without disturbing her so that in the morning when she woke she was surprised first to be in this strange white room and then to see someone else asleep beside her.

Chapter Seven

As the sunlight reached them, Sangito woke and turned to Jean. Their bodies moved into each other. He buried himself inside her, his head between her breasts, his penis thrusting, searching. She felt that he had forgotten who she was, had only a blind need to find her source, but she felt his orgasm as a pleasure, the act of giving all she desired in return for his warmth and sense of being wanted. She bubbled with happiness, laughing and rolling with him over the mattress and onto the floor where they jumped out of bed into the morning.

He watched her dressing, sitting with his back against the wall, keeping his distance. She wanted him to desire her, to find her beautiful. She put on her bra and pants. 'Those knickers aren't sexy,' he said critically. She felt deflated. Fearing he might turn away from her, she replied laughing: 'Oh yes, I buy them to please you, then?' Impudence was her only defence. She wore her independence as a cloak to hide her vulnerability. Even while she stood in front of him, her hands on her hips in mock anger, she worried that her stomach would be too large, would not show the proper curve. She had not told him how old she was. He was thirty, she knew that. How would he feel about her if he knew?

They went out to breakfast, walking hand in hand to the

cafe on the corner, sitting across from each other over greasy eggs and white bread. Soon it would be time for her to join the demonstration which was starting in Trafalgar Square.

'I'll go with you on the bus,' said Sangito. 'I'll get off at Oxford Street, there's a meeting at the centre. Will you be back tonight?'

'Yes, it's my last night. I'll come back as soon as it's over. I want to be with you. Will you be in?'

So it was settled and they sat on the top deck of the bus, looking down on London from the height of their togetherness, feeling the memory of each other in their bodies. Jean held his hand; she felt giddy and silly, her cunt soft and tender, remembering him. He left the bus first, turning at the stairs to smile at her before he went down. She smiled back, her spirits high as she watched his small dark head between the other heads, and then the bus moved on and she lost him.

She was going somewhere too. This demonstration was important to her; it was by her choice that she would be on it. She walked in the crowded streets, strong in her own world, not needing to keep to the wall, not giving way to other people as she usually did. She was a woman with a political purpose; she had a right to be there, to be angry, to demand for herself the freedoms which men took for granted. She was demanding the right to control what went on in her own body. It was late for her to be asking, almost irrelevant, yet she *was* asking and did so together with younger women so that they would never have to endure the dangers she had had to endure. Yes, it had been dangerous. Until now she had never allowed herself to think that: she could have died that morning in the bathroom. She could have curled up on the floor in a pool of blood from a haemorrhage made by the knitting needle thrust into her. Why had she never thought of that? So busy blaming herself for the death of that small body, she had never realised that she too had had rights, could make demands. No one had told her that.

Then she saw the banners and the people. There were so many standing round the fountains and on the steps. She hadn't expected this. She walked past groups of women, past political banners: the communist party, the revolutionary anarchists, neighbourhood groups, playschools, women's aid. She could see no one she knew. How would she ever find Sara? There were thousands of people, everyone in a holiday mood because of the weather: mothers with children, fathers too. She read a banner which said *Women's Liberation: A Woman's Right to Choose*, and made for it. She could join them even if she did not know the women. That was for everyone, she would not be marching under false colours, she thought. But no woman would be doing that today, she reminded herself.

So she stood with a group of strange women. She recognised some of the faces from the women's liberation conference and from the meeting before it. Barbara was there, the woman with the woman's sign on her jeans. Jean smiled at her and went to stand beside her.

'We're leading the march,' insisted Barbara, pulling them all forward. 'There won't be any men leading this march.'

'They should walk at the back,' another woman agreed. 'They won't though. We should make sure that they aren't in front.' Then they were moving off. The group she was with picked up their banner and joined the front of the march where the National Abortion Campaign banner also waved.

'Here,' said Barbara, 'here are some leaflets to give out,' and thrust a pile of typed sheets into Jean's hand.

It was exciting walking up the Haymarket. The police kept the traffic away and she could see the long line of people, mostly women, filling up the road behind them. She walked close to the pavement so that she could give out the leaflets. She gave them to women, smiling and trying to share her feeling with them about the march being her march. Some took the leaflet, others turned their heads away.

'No, I don't want anything to do with you lot,' said an oldish woman walking with another woman, an expression of disgust on her face. Jean shrugged and moved on. She felt enormously alive, her body carrying her over Piccadilly Circus into Regent Street. When she approached couples sauntering on their afternoon shopping spree, she held out the leaflet to the woman, although often the man would lean over and take it from her. 'It's about our right to choose what goes on in our own bodies,' she would say, looking at the woman. Sometimes the response would be embarrassment, or a rejection, but often she was met with a smile in return, and the leaflet would be tucked carefully into a shopping bag.

'What do we want?' shouted a woman in a tweed jacket loudly.

'Abortion on demand, a woman's right to choose,' everyone responded.

'When do we want it?'

'Now!'

At first Jean was unable to shout, but as they approached Oxford Circus she found her voice. 'Abortion on demand!' she shouted, her voice sounding loud and high to her inner ear. The large procession snaked its way up Regent Street, along Oxford Street and into Hyde Park where there was to be live music and a carnival atmosphere. They were among the first to arrive, the 50,000 others took another hour to walk the distance and by that time the music had already started. People split away from the march into groups of friends, chatting. Jean stood for a while with the women who had marched next to her, but they seemed to have plans for the evening, were making arrangements about where to eat, it did not seem as if she was included. It was too early to return to the square, so Jean made a circuitous walk around the crowds. Perhaps she would see Sara, she thought, but she recognised no one. She felt very lonely among all these people, but glad too that she had been part of them, proud that she had marched shouting down the street, a militant at last.

Sangito and Jean drank in the pub after she got back, returning in the yellow lamplight to his room and the mattress on the white painted floor. They had never talked of love and they did not do so now.

'You must send me a card from India,' said Jean. 'I want

one with elephants on it.'

'I'll remember. Perhaps you'll come out too.'

'No, never. I'd go barmy wearing only one colour. Why do you? Because you're told to?'

'No. It isn't like that. Bagwan doesn't wear orange. He wears white. It's my own choice.'

'Why do you then?'

But the answer made no sense to her It didn't matter. They kissed. He held her and put his head in her lap. She felt both involved and distanced by their lovemaking. His use of her body showed his desperate need, but at the same time he made other demands on her which confused her. When he touched her, she felt warm and giving, open to him, but when she stood up to fetch a tissue from her bag, she could see him look at her critically, from the outside, and she closed up, retreated into the body which she presented then as a picture in a magazine, made uneasy by his scrutiny.

'Tell me about your family,' she said when she had settled down again.

'My mother died when I was seven. My father married again. I love him, but he can't take what I do. And she won't let him see me much. When he visits, she sits in the car and won't come in.'

Jean cradled him in her arms, her legs and breasts enclosing him. She wanted to give him everything he was asking for. She wanted to thank him for being there when she needed him, for making her body come alive again after so many dry years.

When she woke in the morning, he was still asleep. She left the bed quietly and went to dress. Today was a day for saying goodbye to the new Jean she had discovered in this short time. She wanted to walk in the city, she wanted to sit next to the river and say goodbye to the London which had given itself to her. When she was ready to go, she kissed Sangito. He stirred and put out his arms to her.

'I'm leaving now. Sleep some more. It's still morning. I'll be seeing you. Thanks.'

'Stay a little longer. Please stay.'

'No. I must go now. Thank you for everything.'

On her way to the tube, she called in at the community

shop. Walter was polishing the brass knocker on the front door as she came up the street.

'I'm going back to Winchester today. Came to say goodbye.'

'You'll be back. Are you coming in for tea?'

'Yes please.'

Janet said: 'Sara was round here yesterday. She was looking for you. She asked if we'd seen you. She seemed worried about you.'

'I've been fine. She needn't have worried. I'll tell her.'

Jean took the tube to Trafalgar Square. When she came up into the air, she found it full of tourists and pigeons. She touched the nearest lion for good luck, and then walked towards the river. Crossing the footbridge, she leaned over the railings to watch a barge drift slowly beneath her and gazed up river at solid grey buildings and the rounded dome of St Paul's. Seagulls swooped across the water. A man and a woman were throwing crusts of bread from the bridge, which the birds caught as the flew. They whirled and screamed as if asking for more.

It seemed a long time since she had left the mews and yet it was only two days ago. It seemed a long time since she had seen Sara. I should have said goodbye – I'll write, she promised herself. But what claimed her attention the most was the sense that she was becoming someone else. Returning to Winchester was like putting on old clothes that she had discarded or covering a plant that was growing.

She crossed the river and sat for a while on a bench, looking back. She did not want to leave. The seagulls' cry echoed her own pleasure and pain. In the distance, against the sky line, the post office tower, like a signpost, told her where she had come from that morning. I will return to London, she promised herself.

It was time to catch the train. Her mother would be wanting to hear about her two weeks on her own. It was time also to work out how she would live from now on. She had been shown another way. It was up to her to make that direction her own.

She walked towards Waterloo Station. As she passed the suburban overground railway line, she noticed neat white

writing high up on the brick wall.
     ABORTION KILLS, it said, WOMEN MURDER BABIES.

Autumn

Chapter Eight

2 River Lane,
St Cross.
Winchester.
3rd August.

Dear Sara,

I send you sisterly greetings from this fat English countryside. Have been gardening solidly since I saw you – my mother's garden needs such a lot of loving work. No, that isn't quite true, I've been reading too and lust after more conversations with you about 'production and reproduction', sexism reaching through the family and winding us all into tightly bound cocoons, and we ourselves spinning the web which keeps us bound. I remember you sitting on your brown bed and saying: 'Be true to yourself,' and I wonder whether I will ever find out who I am so that I can be! What I became in London is still with me, I haven't forgotten, nor have I forgotten the warmth of your friendship and I thank you for it. By the way I heard from Janet that you had been out looking for me, that you feared I wouldn't be able to look after myself! Don't worry, I was fine and went on the march and looked and looked for you, but couldn't find you. It was an amazing march, didn't you think so? I had a good time handing out leaflets to the women shopping and had quite a few conversations with women in the street, who said they were with us. As well as a few insults!

My job hunting has gone well. Did you get the note I put through the door after the interview? I called at the mews on my way back to the train, but no one was in. Anyway, I've been offered four sessions a week at the Waterloo Project for a six month period, starting first September – which is why I'm writing really, as I haven't found a place to stay as yet. Do you know of a space down the street? Or in the Square? I should be most grateful if you could spread the word. I'll probably want to come up around the 27th to settle in. Not too sure what the work entails, there is a youth club and a cafe on the premises and I have to help with them, but the main thing is an Intermediate Treatment group being set up for adolescent girls for six months only. You've probably heard of IT, it's a new way of spending money on young people who've got into trouble with the courts or who've been referred by social services because they are truanting or something. Sounds like a lot of work for one or two sessions, and a cheap way of keeping young people under control when they can't make them go to school. But setting up groups for girls only is something very new, and I feel I have something to say and something to learn there.

They are cutting the hay in the fields around us and the golden squares are scattered across the hillsides. Why don't you come down to visit? I'd be so pleased to see you and we could go up St Catherine's Hill with a bottle of cider and two boiled eggs and just sit and dream in the sun. Please come. In sisterhood,
Jean.

The letter brought Sara down the following weekend. She arrived mid-afternoon on Friday, her baggage a plastic bag with a change of clothes and two books.

'I'd like to take you home along the river. Do you mind if we walk?'

'Oh no, I was smelling the hay as we came down. What a change from London air, I miss it so much.'

Jean was self-conscious walking next to Sara. Feeling responsible for her friend she felt compelled to point out the cathedral, the college. Jeremy would have called it 'Mom's guided tour', but she didn't know how else to bridge the silences. The path was narrow and they often bumped against each other, their bodies awkward, needing to get used to being together again.

'Let's sit down here and look at the water meadows.' It was one of Jean's favourite places, a bench strategically placed so that it looked over a small stream and the flat expanse of water meadows to a steep hill marked by ancient earth-works and crowned with circle of beech trees.

'We're nearly at my mother's house, but I like being here. It's so lovely looking across the bullrushes and flags. Even the cows look smug. Well I suppose they have reason to be.'

*　　　*　　　*

Sara was silent, just looking. She had come down because she felt bruised and needing comfort, but now she was here she didn't know how to ask for it. She wanted to say: 'I'm so frightened Dave will leave me,' but she was unable to, not only because she was ashamed to say it, but also because if she did say it, she might perhaps have to face the reality of it happening, of truly being left by him.

She wanted to say: 'I think I may be pregnant,' but she didn't say that either. It was too soon to tell anyway, so why should she be? There was only this vague fear inside her, her body uneasy; she listened to it and thought, I'll wait until the first week in September and then I'll go for the test. It's too soon now. It's stupid to think it might happen, I'm only a couple of days overdue.

She said: 'Why are they called water meadows?' Although her father had taught her to recognise almost all the common wild flowers, today the landscape was a blur to her, nothing but shades of different greens with a dash of yellow or purple – yes, that was willow herb – the knowledge was just reaction. She took no pleasure in it; the pain inside was too great for her to look outwards as well.

Jean laughed as she replied. 'I've never thought about it.

They are boggy though, and there are a lot of little canals which drain them. You can't just walk across, you keep on coming up against streams that are too wide to jump over. I hope we'll do a lot of walking while you are here. I love to be out in the meadows and it's better when there's someone with me, although that isn't often. None of my family walk.'

'Tell me about the mews,' she went on. 'How is everyone? Is Don still working so hard? And how is Dave? I'm not cross with him, you know. It's not necessary, no harm came to me. If I'd stayed I should have felt angry. That's why I left.'

'Don's away. He's gone to a fair to sell his shoes. He'll be away a month, and Dave's been very busy with his political work. They're organising a conference on Ireland, and they have to print the newspaper each week and distribute it. He's out most of the time, but he usually comes back two or three times a day, just to see me. It's as if I'm some kind of security for him.'

'Do you feel lonely when he isn't there?'

'No. I've been reading a lot. I've brought you a new novel I've just finished. It's marvellous.'

She didn't say how much it cost her to be alone all day, waiting for him, She didn't say how often she had longed to die when she felt he would not return. Throughout the time she was with Jean, she talked continually about Dave and how much he needed her. She spoke about it after they had had tea and were sitting on the grass with their backs against the grey stone wall of St Cross Hospital, ancient almshouses built close to the river, or when they walked further through an avenue of lime trees and along a river path to the disused railway viaduct, its red brick mellowing into the green fields; now that it was no longer functional it had taken on the look of an ancient monument. They came home in the lightly dark, the shapes of the trees on the path ahead becoming dimmer, the street lights shining over the road to Mrs Gardner's house where Jean's mother waited for them, looking anxiously out of the front room window to see whether they would return before it was truly dark.

'You two had me worried,' she said. She was a small lively woman with a mass of curly white hair and a face which was browned by the sun during her many hours outside tending her plants. Jean loved to see her in the garden; she wore sensible Marks and Spencer shoes and a green anorak while she looked after her abundant flowers and growing vegetables, feeding them with compost and water as if they were her children. She was concerned with appetites, accustomed to providing.

'I've got some cocoa ready for you both, it just needs warming up. And there are scones in the oven. You must be hungry after your walk.'

'And tired,' said Jean. 'I haven't walked so far for ages. Sara will make me fit again. We plan to be out all day tomorrow.'

Sara said nothing, feeling her way in this strange house. She had needed to get away from the strain of loving Dave, yet now she was here she wanted so badly to be with him again. It was as if she ceased to be alive when she no longer saw him, or when she could no longer even expect him to come into the room, bringing with him his vitality and the image of herself which she clung to, Dave's lover, Dave's woman, the person he came home to.

'I think I'll go to bed now. Thank you for the cocoa.' With her head held slightly forward, she moved shyly from the room leaving mother and daughter alone.

'She's very young,' said Mrs Gardner.

'Oh mother, she's still a stranger here. Don't judge already.'

Jean felt annoyed at her mother for saying this, for pointing out the great difference in their ages. It was true, and it hurt because she knew so many people would think what Mrs Gardner had said. How could she argue that in a meeting two people could see each other not as the world saw them? How can anyone know, on a voyage of discovery, who is the most travelled?

The next day they walked further, pausing only to peel an orange or to look at a view. They walked up the hill outside the city and over it, across a valley overgrown with knee-high nettles and beyond it, skirting cultivated barley fields, where the larks circled singing above their heads. It seemed as if Sara wanted to exhaust herself and Jean was glad to keep pace with her, their bodies browning in the strong sun, their jeans feeling too hot and constricting for such a long walk.

They bought cans of beer and bread and cheese from a village shop and sat next to the river, picnicking.

'Don't you feel left out of Dave's world sometimes?' asked Jean curiously.

'Well, only when he gets angry with me. Did I tell you that Don and I did portraits of each other and him on the walls?'

'No. Go on.'

'You know if you stand against a wall and someone traces your outline, there is a kind of shadow portrait of you. Don and I traced each other, and then we wanted one of Dave. He was on his way out, but he got into it and stood for a moment on the stairs while we drew round him. Then he was off, and we felt like taking the piss out of him, so we wrote: "Has the revolution begun yet, Dave?" on the wall next to it. We only meant it as a joke.'

She stopped for a moment, picking at the ground near her knee, where a small tuft of grass and a few silvery leaves grew tightly together.

'Was he angry?'

'Terribly. He was furious!' She laughed uncomfortably. 'Don and I were sitting on the cushions having coffee when he came up the stairs and saw it and came into the room in a rage. He stood towering above us, the two of us crouched down, looking up at him. He said we wouldn't even know if there *was* a revolution and if it didn't happen it would be our fault anyway!' There was another pause. Jean looked at Sara's hands which were still busy demolishing the grass. 'He calmed down after a while and the picture is still up. You'll see it when you come again. He doesn't really mean to be like that, it's just his enthusiasm.'

'I know. And he's marvellous to be with. He does make you feel as if the revolution will really happen.'

'I sometimes feel my life started with him.'

'Yes.'

They were silent, not wanting to get up, unwilling to leave

the river.

'It's hot enough to swim,' suggested Jean. 'There's no one about. Let's jump in.'

The bank shelved slowly into the shallow water. Sara flopped in with a splash, swimming across to where a tangle of water plants formed a raft on the swift current. There was nothing for it: Jean fell in as well, both of them gasping from the cold, their skin pink from the water.

'If you lie on your back, the current floats you along,' said Jean. 'I have the feeling if I'm not careful I'll end up naked in the next town, with only a few water weeds to cover me.'

Sara gulped water and laughed. 'Not even dead – like Ophelia!'

They were shy with each other when they got out. Not looking at their bodies they dried themselves quickly on the T-shirts they were about to put on. Jean shivered a little. 'Let's walk again – that was cold.'

'We talk a lot about men, don't you think?' said Jean when they had regained their breath and were on a narrow path which was overgrown with brambles. Sara was holding up a long thorny branch so that she could get through without catching her clothes. Sara walked faster than she did and she felt she needed to talk to draw them together.

'What do you mean?' Sara was ahead of her throwing the words back over her shoulder.

'Well, when we're alone we talk about Dave and, oh, I don't know, it's as if who we are depends on who they are.' They climbed over a stile and the path widened so they could walk together again. 'You know, perhaps we should say how men should be, just as they always tell us how we should be.'

'We do,' said Sara. 'I do, anyway. I always look for a certain type of man. I like men who know where they are going, assertive men. I don't think they're much good for me though.'

'Do you remember Clive, the gentle hippy guy who lives down the street? Don't you like him then?'

'No,' Sara was quite definite. 'I think he's weak and feeble somehow. Droopy. He gives me the shivers.'

'But that's unfair. We always say we want men to be more like us, to be more sensitive, gentler, less dominant. We say we want to stop stereotypes and then you judge Clive according to the stereotypes after all.'

'I know. I can't help it.'

'Well, I like him. I can talk to him, and I hardly know him. When he came to the mews I had quite a long conversation with him. Most men frighten me. I feel judged. And graded F – oh, these lovely flowers! Tell me what this one is called.'

She picked a tall purple spike. Sara said that was purple loosestrife and Jean kept it, gradually gathering more flowers until she had a whole bunch; watermint, willow herb, meadowsweet, agrimony. The names were nothing like the tamer names of garden flowers; they seemed magical, as if they were part of some ancient hidden knowledge that Sara was passing on to her.

The next morning there was a telephone call for Sara.

'It's someone called Monica,' said Mrs Gardner and Jean turned quickly away from the tea she was making to watch Sara hurry to the telephone. She was soon back, standing white-faced in the doorway.

'Mark asked her to phone.' she said, looking at Jean. 'Dave's moved out. He's left the mews in such a mess that Mark keeps falling over things and has gone home until it's tidied up. We've been together for two years, sharing most things, so I expect he found it difficult to get his stuff out without disturbing mine.' She tried to laugh. 'I'll have to go back at once.'

Jean looked at the clock. 'You've just missed a train. There's another one in an hour. I'll go with you to the station. You've got time to have breakfast.'

Chapter Nine

Sara stood at the top of the stairs and looked into the living room of the mews. She had to lean forward slightly, holding onto the door frame because her way was blocked by a jumble of books and suitcases and clothes, most of which she recognised as her own. The living room looked as if a tidal wave had hit it. The bookshelves had been pulled off the wall and lay crookedly under the books they had once carried, as if Dave had changed his mind once they were down and had decided not to take any books after all. Not surprising, she thought wryly, they were mine anyway.

Sara felt ill seeing the mess. The destruction appeared to her malevolent. She felt she was stepping into a sphere of violence which threatened her very existence. This was where she lived, these things, thrown about the room were her possessions, her life. That was her black velvet dress which now lay crumpled under a pile of old newspapers, a cup of coffee spilled over it hardening into a brown crust. This was her collection of poems by Sylvia Plath which she had bought in her final year at school, now the volumes lay scattered and open under a pile of shoes. She had not even entered her own room and already the destruction of her life was displayed in front of her.

She put her hand to her face and was surprised to see

that it was wet. She was so numb with shock that she hardly paused to think about what she was feeling. She had to find out what further damage had been done and she climbed over several aluminium pots and a canvas stretcher into her own room.

Dave had simply swept clear every shelf and drawer, every surface or ledge and piled it all into the middle of the room, from whence he had proceeded to extract those things which he thought were his. Needing a container, he had grabbed a small box and begun to pack and then had seemed to give up half way. His sense of hurry had created this chaos, had turned the room into a disaster area. Sara noticed, as she looked at her tumbled clothes, her records spilled out of their box, her eyes moving slowly over every inch of what she had once called home, that on the window ledge stood a yellow chrysanthemum in full bloom.

Monica: she must have come over to see what it was like and had bought the plant to give her some kind of welcome. Sara fled. It wasn't until she held a mug of tea in her shaking hands and found herself sobbing on Monica's shoulder that she was conscious of her dash out of the mews and across the street to number 76 where Monica lived with her son and several other people. 'I don't even know if I locked the door,' she wailed and stared numbly at her hands while Monica went to check.

'You can stay here tonight,' comforted Monica, 'and when you feel better Nicky and I will help you clear up. I've just been given an electric drill by my parents and I'm longing to use it. I'll put up the shelves again for you in no time.'

'I'd like that,' said Sara, calmer now, 'but I want to get started soon, it's only five now. I could go over now, but still sleep here tonight.'

When Dave came, Monica was washing dishes and Nicky was running from the living-room to the bathroom bringing dirty plates and mugs to her. Dave stuck his head around the door and said: ''Lo. Seen Sara?' Sara looked up as he walked into her bedroom. She was folding jumpers into piles to put

70

them back in her cupboard.

'Oh,' he said, sitting down next to her, his arm around her, 'I'm in a terrible rush. I have to give the van back to Maurice tonight and I haven't enought money for petrol to get there. Can you lend me a pound until tomorrow?' He looked briefly around the room. 'I had to move in about two hours, you know. But you must come and see my room, I've got it really nice and Doreen has given me a blue carpet and two plants. It looks amazing. I took one of your posters for my wall, the French one about '68, hope you don't mind.'

Sara looked at him, all her love for him still on her face. If she screamed at him now, what would he think of her? Would he ever return? She couldn't risk that. She managed a small smile. 'I'll come to see it when I've got this sorted out,' she replied. It was the only reproach she could manage, the only one she dared. And he, sensing her withdrawal perhaps, or even sensing her pain, put his arm more tightly round her, fumbled for her breasts and the buttons on her shirt.

'Come on. Don't be sad, it'll be all right, you'll see.' He pulled her over to the mattress, pushing aside the clothes, books, records and magazines that had been dumped on it. He was already unzipping his jeans, throwing them down in an impatient movement with his left hand while his right was taking off her shirt, unbuckling the belt on her trousers.

Sara didn't know what she wanted, but it wasn't this. She was afraid, however, that this was all she would get and she settled for it as a hungry person might for a piece of rancid meat. She felt stunned, her mind registering what Monica was doing in the next room; she could hear her call to Nicky to bring her some more mugs and to empty the ash-trays. Dave didn't have time to help, he had said, and here she was lying under him while her neighbour cleaned her house. She moved her body to Dave's rhythm, not because she felt any passion, but because she wanted him to come quickly so that it would all be over soon. There would be time later to work out how she felt, and time too for Dave to go or stay as he wished. She was afraid, though, to admit that she knew he would rather be with his new friends than with her.

With a small grunt Dave collapsed onto her. Giving her

71

a quick hug, he withdrew his penis and started to put on his clothes. She lay as he had left her, looking at him.

'Where did you say the pound was?' he asked as he wriggled into his jeans. 'I've got to go soon. I'll make some coffee,' and he was out of the room, closing the door behind him.

Sara felt too bruised to move. She could hear him talking to Nicky, asking him what he was doing, and then his voice faded and mingled with the sound of running water and Monica's voice. He had been in the house for less than ten minutes. She felt wet between her legs and the smell of semen was very strong. She would have to clean herself, she thought, as she sat up and looked around for the knickers she had been wearing. Wiping Dave's seed off her thighs, and pulling back the lips of her vagina to make sure it was all clean, she imagined, with a tremor, another person, half Dave, growing inside her. This would be a part of himself he wouldn't be able to take away, who would need her and stay with her. And perhaps if Dave liked the baby, he'd want to stay too.

It was crazy to think like that, she told herself, tucking her shirt into her jeans. No one would think it was a good idea. Her parents would certainly disapprove and it would give them just the reason they wanted to come down and carry her back home. To make matters worse, she wouldn't be able to do without them then. Dave would never really help. Even now, when she was on social security, he borrowed money from her. And his political work would suffer. It was selfish to want someone when there was a whole world that needed changing. And he *did* love her, he *did* always come back, even if only for a minute. Maybe if she just waited, it would be all right. No, she didn't want to be pregnant, that was for sure. If that happened too much would change too quickly. Oh why, she wished, isn't there any blood?

When Dave had gone, the two women worked together again, just cleaning and tidying, but Nicky was tired and whiney and Monica said she had to go home to give him his tea.

'I'll come with you,' said Sara. 'I can't stay here on my

own. I'll finish this tomorrow. I want to phone Mark to tell him I'm back and fixing things up and I'll phone Jean too to tell her Dave's room is empty; she's looking for a place. I don't think Mark or Don will mind, they both like her.'

Thinking of Jean coming to live at the mews made her feel more secure. Sara liked the way they talked together and Jean seemed to accept who she was without wanting to change her, like her parents did. She felt more experienced talking with her than she did with other people, and Jean was her friend, not Dave's, not one of Dave's amazing women friends whom he held up to her as examples of what she ought to become – politically committed, strong feminists. She didn't have the confidence to challenge Dave's image of them and was too over-awed when she was with them to tell them how she was feeling. It was different with Jean, they seemed more equal, she even sometimes felt she was the stronger. Maybe with someone like that in the mews she would have the courage to go out more and to work out what she wanted to do.

But she still felt numb, as if she were existing only at a very small level of her being, as if the rest of her had been blown away by a landmine. She did not yet ask: 'What is he doing to me?' but held herself together as much as she could and walked away from the mews, locking the door behind her, her toothbrush, a book and her purse held tightly in her hand.

Chapter Ten

Stephen was on the phone to Jean.

'So . . . I hear you are moving to London.'

'Yes, that's right. I've got a part-time job as a youth worker.'

'Part-time? Will you have enough money? Do you want me to send you some?'

'Thank you, no. I'll have enough.'

Jean instantly mistrusted this solicitude. Why was he phoning, why was he offering money? She hadn't heard from him since May, and suddenly just when she was about to leave, there was this offer. His voice, deep and strong, always made her feel like a silly woman, as if she was bound to be in the wrong whatever she did. Her hand tightened on the telephone receiver, she stiffened, wary.

'Jeremy tells me you'll be living with a whole lot of his drop-out friends . . .'

'I'm sure he never said it like that.'

'No, but that's what they are, out of work layabouts and in a' – his voice took on a curl of distaste – 'squat.'

'It's not like that . . .' began Jean.

'Don't tell me what it's like. I know those kinds of places. Filthy, disease ridden. You'll be in trouble with the police if you stay there. Why don't you let me give you something so you can get yourself a decent place.'

'No, really, it's not like that at all. They are my friends. I want to stay there. I shall have a very comfortable room.'

'Look Jean, I know you, you get taken in by people. They're half your age, filled with all that youthful radical fervour. You're too old for that. It doesn't suit you, and besides it's dangerous.'

'Stephen, you must let me live my own life. This is where I want to live. I do appreciate your concern, but I'm not in any danger, really.'

'Jean, I'm phoning you for your own good. You take my advice and look for a little bed-sit somewhere in Battersea, they're quite reasonable there I'm told, and I'm sure you'll make other friends in no time.'

'I don't want other friends. These people suit me. I'm changing a lot, Stephen, I'm not the woman you knew four months ago. You don't know what's best for me.'

'Jean, I think you are being most unreasonable. Here am I, worrying about you —'

'But you needn't!'

'All the same, I do, and offer you a way to get reasonable accommodation —'

'But —'

'Let me finish. Reasonable accommodation, and you persist in staying with these most unsuitable —'

'They aren't, they're my friends.'

'Look, you're probably going through some kind of menopausal madness, but you have to consider your family as well. Surely I don't have to spell it out. Say you were arrested, or there was some kind of scandal, drugs, I don't know what, you've got Jeremy to consider and your mother, even if you don't care about yourself.'

Jean's voice became cold and hard. She saw now what he was doing and it hadn't helped that he had tried to make her feel ridiculous by mentioning her age.

'Stephen, when I want your advice, I'll ask for it. I should think you would be the last person to presume to tell me how to behave. Thank you for your offer of help. And don't worry, what I do won't harm you; I've been using my maiden name and no one knows anything about you.'

'Now, don't take it like that . . .' his voice blustered on but she wasn't listening any more. She waited for the end of a sentence.

'Well, thanks for calling. I'll send you a card with my address. Goodbye.'

Mrs Gardner was sitting on the lawn under the yew tree with the tea cups and teapot ready to pour. She was reading when Jean came out to join her.

'Bloody Stephen, what gives him the right –' she fumed as she plumped herself down on the waiting deck chair and helped herself to a cup of tea.

Mrs Gardner looked over her glasses. 'Stephen?'

'He's just phoned, wants to pay for a flat in bloody Battersea so I won't disgrace him by squatting. MEN. All they think about is themselves, and their reputations. He acts as if I still belong to him and he can tell me what to do.'

'Perhaps he was being kind.'

'Kind? Stephen? My first bit of freedom, my first chance of changing and he's being kind? They kill us with that kindness. It's like their respect for women which forces us to be eternally feminine and forever the slaves to their master race.'

She waved her cup around and spilled her tea. 'Damn,' she muttered, wiping her shirt with a tissue from her sleeve.

Mrs Gardner looked sad. She had been one of the first women to graduate from Cambridge University, although even then she had been refused an actual degree, having to content herself with a certificate to say that she had passed the examination which would have allowed her the use of the title MA Cantab, if she had been a man. The degree had been awarded to her some years later, but by that time she had married a fellow student, who became the kind country vicar who was Jean's father. Five years ago, after his death, she had settled in this small house in Winchester, devoted herself to the garden and never again gone to church. It was as if she was saying that she could be firm about what she wanted, but would not harm anyone else by doing it.

She looked at Jean. 'I read that book you gave me on housework, and the poems.'

'Yes?'

'They are right, I think, but not very nice women. Not generous.'

'But Mother, they are angry and they have the right to be. We have been denied so much, told to be satisfied with marriage and children, never allowed to find out who we really are.'

'I know, I agree, but life isn't always about discovering things and being happy. It's also about sacrifice and suffering. There is something about enduring pain that brings out the best in people. To me it's as if women have always provided that quality of goodness in the world, as if we redeem it somehow.'

'Maybe if we'd been allowed to have some share in running it, it wouldn't need redemption.'

'That could be. But the way those women talk, it's just shrill anger, hate and spite. I don't think that's much good.'

'Look Mother, you told me you were much cleverer than Dad, yet you put all your energy into him, into making him comfortable and proud of himself. What about what you wanted?'

'That was what I wanted. Oh I don't say I wasn't fed up sometimes and impatient when he did things I didn't believe in, but he was a good man. I suppose I was lucky.'

Jean wanted to go on and say: 'And I suppose I wasn't', but there didn't seem much point in arguing. She looked round at the late summer roses and the fruit trees laden with apples, like carvings on an elaborate wooden screen and smiled wryly. She hadn't had the attention her mother had given so devotedly to her father. It had been assumed that she would imitate the example of womanhood demonstrated to her, and she had done so. Now it was late and hard to strike out on her own and for herself alone. She needed the support of all those angry articles and poems; she needed other women to join with her in a bitter harangue against what was expected of them. But for her mother it was too late to change. Dad would say that she had cast her bread on the waters, thought Jean, and she looked lovingly at her mother as she got up stiffly and picked up her pruning scissors to cut away the unruly holly that was swamping the vegetable patch in the far corner of the garden where the blackberries were still ripening.

When she travelled up to London Jean carried not only a very large suitcase, but also a bag of plants for the mews and for Janet. There were the herbs she had promised, thyme and mint, sage and rosemary as well as a deep blue geranium which would survive the winter cold and grow into a big clump the following summer. She intended to plant them in a window-box on the roof, where Cocaine couldn't nibble at them. She took a taxi to the mews and hugged Mark when he opened the door. 'It's me, Mark, I'm back! It feels like I've come home. Will you let me in?' He laughed and helped her with her things.

'You've just missed Sangito. He called yesterday and asked when you'd be up. He's going to India today I think.'

'Oh well, I'll see him when he gets back. I can't believe you're awake though. It's not even afternoon yet. What's happened?'

'Didn't Sara say? I'm training as a counsellor for handicapped people. I go to college every day. Today I'm writing an essay, otherwise I'm usually first out of the house because I've a long way to travel. But everyone is busy now.'

Things had certainly changed. Sara was working for a large trades union, she was one of three workers in the basement who did all the mailing and printing and duplicating. Don had been taken on as an apprentice for a Bond Street shoe firm who made elegant hand-made shoes for wealthy customers. The mews was empty now during the day; it was quiet when Jean got up, only the hurriedly stacked breakfast things telling her that the others had eaten and gone. She, in contrast, had time to read the paper and make her bed and wash up the dirty plates, loving again the space she shared with these new friends and in which she felt so at home.

Jean's work started later in the day. Every Tuesday evening she helped at a youth club, selling sweets and keeping a watchful eye out for any trouble, although she had no idea what she would do if there were any. The young people were of all ages, eight year olds to eighteen, all of them heavy smokers, who would not hesitate to steal her cigarettes if she left them lying around, yet at the same time improvidently generous with their own, always offering her one if they lit up while talking to her. She wondered where they got the money to smoke so much, but when she asked, they were vague, smiled, spoke of Saturday jobs and free fags from the corner shop. They were very different from the boys in the preparatory school in which she had taught when she was married and her relationship with them was different. She had no school hierarchy to give her authority, she had no power; but, at the same time, they were more open with her. She was learning from them how hard it was to be young round Southwark, with little to do and not much to look forward to, and now that the nights were closing in, it wasn't so easy to hang around the flats or play football in the vacant lot around the corner.

But where were the girls? she wondered. A few came to the club; they were carefully dressed, their hair combed meticulously in place, but they looked at Jean with disdain when she tried to talk to them. They had come to be seen and talked to by the boys, not by this middle-aged bag. What would they have in common with her, their faces said plainly. Their youth was brittle, fragile, it was all they had, and they suspected that even now with the little experience of life that they had. They could achieve happiness only by being noticed for it, their brightly coloured exteriors covered carefully hidden emotions, flattened down to fit their circumstances.

So the girls made up only a small percentage of the young people who came to the club. John, the senior worker, talked about that to Jean and to Paula, who was to be her co-worker in the all-girls IT group. Paula was a young and energetic woman who had worked in women's centres in other cities and who was clearer than Jean about the need for feminism in youth work.

'All girls need separate girls' groups,' she argued with John. 'Look how few come to the youth clubs. There's nothing for them here, just like there's nothing for them outside. All they do here is watch the boys. IT spends most of its money on boys because it's boys who make trouble.

Girls don't even think to rebel. And you give us six months to get a group going. Six months! It's ludicrous.'

But although John agreed with her, the decision had been made elsewhere. Six months was what they had been allocated. He explained that they would be given names of likely girls by Social Services and Educational Welfare. They would have to keep records of money spent on the workers and on the girls, reports would have to be written and each girl would have to be visited at home to ask her whether she would want to join the group.

There was a lot of paper work: letters had to be written, phone calls made to all kinds of statutory bodies. In the end they had twenty-two names of girls who were considered to be at risk. What would they do with them if they did come? Jean and Paula spent hours discussing that too, but felt unable to decide before the girls themselves made their own demands. Friday was the day on which this group would meet, and it was the day on which these discussions took place. Jean always felt exhausted on Saturdays, yet she had not yet met a single member of the group. Time was running out, they were to be employed for six months only. She and Paula set the fifth of October as the date for the first meeting and divided the names between them. They had two weeks to visit the girls in order to convince them that such a group would be worth joining. Not one of them went to school regularly; Jean could not imagine what would entice them to make a long journey on a Friday afternoon to meet with two strange women and a few other girls they did not even know. Dutifully she made arrangements with social workers who would go with her to the housing estate where each girl lived, or who would make appointments for her to go alone. She learned from these calls that in the time that she and Paula had been collecting the names, five of the original twenty-two had disappeared from sight, dropped through the net that Social Services and the other institutions had spread around them. It was a large percentage, which made Jean ponder the risk which she had talked about so glibly. Where were they? They were under age and could not work without national insurance numbers, they were not at home and had no access to money. Or did they? The streets were full of predators, waiting for their sex. She hoped at least that they were in control of what was happening to them. If that were possible.

Chapter Eleven

Mark and Jean walked down to the hospital together to visit Sara. It wasn't far enough away to take a bus even though it was raining. Mark held a black umbrella over them and Jean carried his stick under her arm. The weather had broken earlier in the week and it seemed as if the rain would never stop; it pounded against the trees which were already turning colour and filled up the pavements and gutters with soggy yellow leaves. They sounded pleasant as you walked through them, muffling the noise of boots on hard stone, but it was a nuisance always coming back with wet feet and dripping raincoats, or sitting all day with a chill round your ankles because of your damp trousers.

Sara was in bed when they reached her ward. The notice on the door said: *Termination*, which made Jean shudder. She thought Sara looked very small and alone. Only one other bed was occupied, also by a young, tense woman. Jean pulled Mark along with her so that they surrounded the bed. 'We've brought chocolates and look, pink carnations!' she exclaimed as Sara managed to pull a smile across her white face.

*　　　*　　　*

Sara had wanted so badly to keep the baby. She knew it was impossible: she would lose her job, have no money, was only eighteen, but she wanted it, more than anything out of a sense of despair. It was as if all the meaning had drained out of her life. Dave was visiting less and less, she could feel his interest in her slipping away. He came round now only if he was in the neighbourhood, hardly ever with the express purpose of seeing her, and when he did, he would eat a meal or borrow money without really talking to her. To Sara it seemed that he showed more interest in Don or Jean than he did in her, as if their opinion of him mattered more to him than hers did. She felt wiped out of existence now, erased from life; she couldn't see the point of the little daily things one did to stay alive – washing, eating, even working at her new job. She did all of them with an underlying awareness of the emptiness inside her. Now she was having an abortion, the word was like a sore in her mouth.

She looked at Jean who was talking about her visits to the estates round Lambeth and Southwark, but her mind ran its own film of Jean sitting across from her at a coffee bar not so long ago, although it seemed now, in this sterile hospital atmosphere, like another world. Jean was looking at her in that other time and saying: 'You can have it, you know. You have the right. Remember, a woman's right to choose doesn't just mean the right to have an abortion, it means that we can *have* children if we want them. We decide, no one else.'

'But it isn't really possible is it?' she had replied, her eyes pleading.

'We could make it possible if you really want it. We could all help, Don and Mark would help too, I'm sure. And I would. You must be sure though, and then if you are, we will give you support. You could live on social security. Monica does it.'

Sara had thought of her parents, but didn't mention them. An illegitimate baby would not go down well in their circle. She would be cutting herself off from them. She looked at Jean and thought that the support she was offering would never be enough. She smiled: 'Thanks. I have to decide soon.'

For there was the pressure of time too, doctors didn't like doing abortions after sixteen weeks, and it must be already eight. Her nerves jangled. Without Dave's love, how could she manage? Yet the baby was half Dave, she could imagine it looking like a small, chubby version of him. How could she get rid of someone who would grow up to be a person like that?

Her mind switched from the past to the present. Jean was saying something about the flowers.

'Yes, they are lovely. Thank you. You can get a vase over there and there's water in the bathrooms.' She wasn't ill, why did she let Jean do all the messing about with the water while she sat up in bed as if she couldn't use her legs? She made up her mind to get up when a young male doctor came in suddenly and asked Mark to wait outside the ward while he did a brief examination. He pulled the curtains around the bed with a rattle of metal rings.

* * *

Jean and Mark stood in the passage.

'I wish I'd brought cigarettes, I'd smoke one now,' grumbled Jean. 'Do you think it's dangerous?'

'No. I've heard people say it is one of the safest forms of contraception now that they're finding out all the things the pill does to women.'

'Not pleasant though.'

'No.'

They stood for a while in silence.

'I'm going drinking after this with friends who used to be with me at college. Want to come?' asked Mark.

But Jean felt too bleak to contemplate meeting new people. She felt like curling up in bed with a hot water bottle and a cup of cocoa. She couldn't bear the idea of leaving Sara in this echoing ward.

Ten minutes before visiting time was over, Dave rushed up the stairs and through the door. He looked flushed and wet, his hair sleek from the rain. 'I've brought you some grapes,' he said, not kissing Sara. 'They've got a bit squashed. I've got a bike now and I had to put them in a carrier bag with all my books and things.' He hauled out a damp paper bag with a small bunch of grapes.

Sara said nothing. She smiled at him. Jean started to put on her coat. 'We'll be off then. Do you want us to visit tomorrow?'

'Yes please. The doctor says I'll feel fine in the evening. I'll probably walk back on Wednesday morning.' Jean kissed her briefly. She hoped Dave would be kind. She and Mark left together. Dave sat down next to the bed to talk to Sara, his hand absentmindedly picking at grapes.

'I've borrowed this book from Doreen for you. It's about women in Vietnam. It's fantastic what they've done, how they've changed. Before the liberation they were treated like animals, even sold as wives to boy children so that he would always have an unpaid servant, and then later, when a man grew up he could marry another woman as well.'

'Thanks. I'll be glad to read it.'

'Don't forget to give it back though. Doreen said to send her love and she hopes you'll come over to the house soon.'

*   *   *

Sara couldn't help remembering her last visit to that house with a sharp cramp of pain. She had gone to the public call box on the corner to phone Dave. She hadn't seen him for a fortnight and now that the pregnancy was confirmed, she had wanted to tell him. She asked if she could come over.

When she had told him, Dave had stood up and moved over to the far corner of the room. She had felt the space beween them as if it were snow. He stood looking out of the window throwing his voice in clipped syllables over his shoulder.

'You are going to have an abortion, aren't you?'

'I don't know. I wanted to know how you feel. Perhaps —'

'How *I* feel? What do I have to do with it?'

'Well, it's yours and I felt somehow that you might want

me to keep it.'

'Why? I don't want to look after a child. I'm nineteen, I've committed myself to revolutionary struggle, how can you think I'd want to cope with a baby?'

'No, I didn't mean it like that. I meant I would look after it, of course.'

'Sara, what are you doing to me? How could you expect that I would want you to have my child? I want to decide things like that, not have them thrust on me in such a sneaky way.'

'I've not been sneaky, I didn't get pregnant on purpose.'

At the idea that she had schemed to become pregnant, Sara began to cry. The tears ran down her cheeks, appearing without any decision on her part. She brushed them away with her right hand.

She felt in her pockets for a tissue. She had been so nervous about telling Dave that she hadn't even taken off her coat. She blew her nose, but the tears continued to fall. She couldn't control them. She wished she hadn't come, could think of no reason why she should stay, yet couldn't get up the momentum to leave. She looked at Dave's back, his shirt without a collar, his lumpy grey jumper with the holes at the elbows. She knew all his clothes, remembered that he had worn that same jumper when they had been truanting from school and had sneaked off to a friend's house, and how they had all sworn to live together in France and be artists and live off the land. She supposed that was why she had gone to France after A levels, hoping that Dave would follow her. He had come, then, but had persuaded her to return. This time he kept his distance.

'I can't take this, Sara. I'm going out.'

He put on his coat and left the room. She could hear him talking to Doreen on the stairs and then the front door banged and the house was quiet. She sat until it was too dark to see in the room. She would have to go, she knew, before Dave returned, but she couldn't move.

Doreen knocked and then quickly put her head round the door.

'I've made supper. Do you want some?' She shivered. 'God, it's cold in here. Come downstairs, the fire's on and there's no one else about.'

Sara had felt comforted by Doreen's concern. She had not realised she was so cold. She sat shivering in front of the gas fire. 'He's a sod, you know,' said Doreen. 'A complete egoist. I'm only just realising that. But I can also see why you love him. When he wants to he can be so warm and caring.'

'It's not that,' replied Sara. 'I'm pregnant.' She felt her body shake with sobs, as if it was reacting outside her centre, as if part of her was watching all this, aghast at what she was unable to control. Perhaps she felt so helpless because normally she hid her feelings completely; now there was this other person inside her and her body no longer listened to her commands.

'Dave's?'

'Yes.'

'What are you going to do?'

'I don't know. I was asking Dave. He thinks I've done it to trap him.'

'Have you?'

'No. Yes. I don't know. I didn't plan to get pregnant.'

'And now you don't know what to do?'

'No, I don't. Like it's a part of Dave. Maybe all I've got left.'

'Do you think you could use it to keep him?'

'I don't know. How do I know what I think?'

Sara buried her face in her hands and wept. She was finding out too much about herself. Could she really be like this?

'Here, I've made some soup. Don't get up. You can sit there and drink it.'

As Sara drank the soup, she warmed up inside. Doreen said nothing more about the baby, but they talked about Doreen's work with handicapped children and what that meant to her. For the first time she felt Doreen was talking to her without Dave as intermediary. She began to talk about her new job as a printer. 'I like it. I like using the machines. They seem to work for me without messing things up, as if they have a sense of who I am. If anyone else uses them, there's chaos, ink everywhere!'

The two women laughed.

'I want you to come again,' said Doreen. 'I'm giving a party next Saturday. Please come.'

It was weird how that had decided her. As she walked home from the tube, she knew that she would not have the child. Being the mother of Dave's child was too bound up with the pain of loving him. Talking with Doreen she had liked herself a bit better suddenly, which gave her the courage to go on without him.

Sara shook herself a little and smiled at Dave. Had he noticed she hadn't been listening? He didn't seem to, he was talking about his job on the paper.

'– and there was this amazing woman who was so militant. She's been in the CP all her life. She's over seventy now and still carries the banner at demos. I love doing these articles, love meeting people like that and they like my work on the paper. I think they may send me to Portugal next month to do a piece on the land reformers.'

Sara smiled at him. She couldn't think of anything to say.

'Well,' he said, gathering his possessions together. 'I must rush, I have to be at a meeting in five minutes.' He looked at her and then at the table next to her bed. He smiled ruefully. 'Sorry. I seem to have eaten all the grapes, you should have stopped me.'

'It doesn't matter. I'm not hungry. Thanks for coming.'

When Dave had gone Sara suddenly found that she was angry. Even now, even when she was about to have an operation, he still talked only about himself, still expected her to be interested in what was happening to him. What about her? She was caught between two impossible choices; had Dave ever made the slightest attempt to understand that? It would never happen to him, so why should he bother with it.

And what kind of choice was it? Whatever she did, her body was not her own. She had given Dave, and now the doctor, the right to decide what to do with it. What about the times she had let Dave sleep with her even when she knew it wasn't safe, just because he wanted it, because she was afraid to refuse him? A woman's right to choose, she thought bitterly, what a laugh.

The woman in the next bed leaned over. 'I'm Ann. What's your name?' Sara looked at her. Her face was white too, like her own. She had lain quietly reading, or pretending to read, while Dave and the others were there. She had had no visitors.

She smiled. 'I'm Sara,' she answered.

Chapter Twelve

Jean was spending the afternoon visiting girls she hoped would join the group. The bus took her to Selwayn Court, a drab block of flats built near London Bridge before the war. The brick had aged badly, fading to a dirty grey and the windows looked small and uninviting. Amanda's mother was mopping down the concrete balcony in front of her second floor flat.

'Oh, Amanda never goes out,' she said definitely. 'I don't either, being a cripple.'

Jean couldn't see where Mrs Reid had any trouble, but she clucked sympathetically. 'Is Amanda home?' she asked and Mrs Reid responded by calling into the silent flat, down the passage leading from the front door.

'Amanda! Lady here wants to see you.'

Jean gathered that she would not be invited in. The flat gave off a strong smell of bleach and wet linoleum. Amanda came silently to the door, a slim dark-haired girl of around fourteen with eyes that looked past Jean at the balcony wall behind her.

'I've come to ask you to join a girls' group at the Waterloo Project. Look, I've brought a map to show you how to get there. We'll meet on Friday afternoons from four to seven. There'll be two of us running the group, and we want to talk about being a woman in this society and maybe you can tell us what you would like to do as well.' It sounded very lame, she thought, winding down like an old-fashioned gramophone. She couldn't see much response from Amanda, who still looked at the brick wall, a small smile playing around her mouth.

'She only goes out with her cousin Irene. Could she come as well?' asked Mrs Reid.

Jean was eager to reply. 'Of course. That would be fine. We'll start in two week's time. Remember, four o'clock on a Friday. I hope you *will* come.'

Amanda nodded and went inside again. Jean stood for a moment waiting to find the words which would make this visit less of a disaster. Mrs Reid, she calculated, was still in her thirties, because Amanda was seven years younger than Jeremy, yet her legs in the lumpy slippers were all swollen, her body much more bent than most women of her age. Perhaps it was her illness, thought Jean, her sympathy going out to this woman with the tired body, who lived out her life on this drab second floor.

'Will she come to the group?' she asked, trying once more to make sure.

'I dunno. If her cousin wants to, she might. She doesn't go to school you know. Too shy. And she has these terrible periods and also a dreadful itch in her back passage.'

Jean couldn't stay any longer. She was afraid that if she did she might be overwhelmed by this woman and never leave. It was too bad, she thought as she negotiated the narrow stairs which smelled of damp, it would be so good if she could get out. She wanted to wave a wand and transform Amanda into a bright confidence instead of this dead retreat. She looked at herself critically, she wasn't much of a fairy godmother: she was wearing a fur coat which Don had given her. Goodness knows where he had found it, a jumble sale probably. It was a dark orange colour and bald on the shoulders where the fur had worn away. She drew it closer round her as she turned into the main street. There was a cold wind blowing, which picked up the dry air and choked her. She hadn't been much use to Amanda, she thought, she looked all wrong, all untidy, she spoke all wrong with her middle-class accent, and what did all these women's liberation phrases mean to Amanda except more proof of how weird this strange-looking woman was, who wasn't a social worker, or so it seemed, yet she talked like one and wanted something from her. I'll send her a card, thought Jean. Maybe she will come.

Her next stop was Southwell, she looked it up again on her A to Z, squinting at the street names. It meant taking two buses, standing in the wind with other patient travellers, mostly women. She exchanged sighs with the woman standing next to her at the bus stop, but neither of them said anything, each one knew the resigned patience that was needed to wait stubbornly in the cold because there is no alternative. It was twilight before she reached the flats she was looking for. The dim light was enough to read the name: *Windermere*, how inappropriate it sounded. The building was enormous and curled round to the back with more stairways and tarred spaces. When she asked him, a young boy showed her the correct entrance.

The flat was completely dark when she knocked. Jean felt so tired at the thought that she had come all this way in vain that she slumped against the wall, waiting. After what seemed like a very long time, the door was opened by a pretty, plump fourteen-year-old black girl.

'Hello,' said Jean, coming forward. 'I'm Jean. Are you Karen or Sharon?'

'Sharon,' said the girl and flashed her a brilliant smile.

'I think Mr Clark has told you about me and that I would visit this afternoon. I'm from the girls' group at Waterloo, or rather the one we want to start, and he thought you and your sister might like to join. Can I come in?'

Sharon stood aside to let her in and then led the way to the main bedrooom, which was the only lighted room in the flat. The floors were uncarpeted and the place felt chill, although there was a paraffin heater in the bedroom, one of those black cylinders that give off a faint light and a strong smell. There were two people in the bed, both of them entirely covered by the bedspread and blankets, but when she came in one of them emerged. It was Sharon's mother. The other remained covered up throughout her visit, but

Jean supposed it must be Karen.

Mrs Elliot hitched herself up in the bed so that she was sitting up. She was entirely dressed in quite a formal dark blue dress. In spite of her tired and overweight body and her rumpled hair, she was a pretty, middle-aged woman, looking much like Sharon. Sharon sat on a large new trunk next to the bed, moving an alarm clock out of the way to give her room. The trunk was the only other furniture in the room besides the bed. 'Sit down,' said Mrs Elliot, patting the foot of the bed. 'Would you like some tea?' She spoke with a strong West Indian accent. There was nothing Jean wanted more and she drank the strong sweet tea which Sharon made for her while she listened to Mrs Elliot.

Mrs Elliot had come to London with her husband nineteen years before. She had left behind her a small boy of six years whom they had never had the money to bring over, nor had she ever visited her old home again. She wiped away a tear as she talked about her son, who was a man now, twenty-five-years old. She had had other children though, nine in fact, in the first ten years of coming to Britain, though all had died except Karen, who was now fifteen, and Sharon, who was fourteen. Her husband had left her some time ago and she lived with the two girls, surviving on a cleaning job, her child benefit and some help from her social worker.

'It's bad now though, we haven't had the child benefit for five weeks, the office hasn't sent my new book, and we just moved in last week.'

'Is this better than your last place?'

Mrs Elliot wasn't so sure. She had been offered a nicer place, nearer her work, but it had been more expensive and she hadn't dared to take it.'

'Doesn't Social Security pay your rent?'

Mrs Elliot shrugged. 'I don't like to be beholden. I've always worked — for ten years. I clean the offices of the National Coal Board, five o'clock in the morning to eight o'clock. This flat is further away than the one I had. I have to get up earlier and pay 20p busfare instead of 10p. They pay me sixteen pounds a week.' She laughed bitterly. 'Each year they give me a pound a week raise.'

That was the reason for the two alarm clocks in the

room. The second stood on the mantlepiece. The cold
morning shift on the empty bus through the sleeping city. If
I did that work, thought Jean, I know I'd spend the rest of the
day in bed.

Instead she talked about the girls' group and what she
hoped they would do, thinking at the same time how much
she would like Mrs Elliot to come to the group as well. She
hoped Sharon would like the sound of what she was saying.

'We'll meet every Friday and cook a meal together and
sometimes we'll go out, maybe to a film or to the ice rink.
And there's also money for a weekend away somewhere.'

'The girls would like that, wouldn't you Sharon?' said
Mrs Elliot, and Sharon nodded, but, like Amanda, she was
wary, not giving anything away.

Jean took her mug into the kitchen to wash it. It was a
shock to see the shelves entirely bare. Next to the sink was a
small box of tea bags, a packet of sugar and an opened tin of
sweetened condensed milk. There were no vegetables or
fruit in baskets as they had at the mews, and no packets of
half-used rice or beans or spices. The shelves looked as if the
kitchen was not used at all.

'Can I buy you a cake for your new house?' asked Jean as
Sharon walked with her to show her where to catch the bus.
The one-way system made the return trip more com-
plicated than she had expected. 'I didn't know you had just
moved in. I'd like to give you a moving-in present,' and they
turned in to a baker's shop to buy a loaf of sweet madeira
cake.

'I hope you'll come to the group. And bring Karen.'

'Can I bring my friend Joy as well?' asked Sharon.

'Yes,' said Jean, 'Of course.'

The group was forming itself, she thought as she rode
back on the top of the bus. The trouble was going to be to
persuade the very shy girls to come along. Those who had
friends would come in groups, but the solitary girls, who
stayed in the shadow of their homes, would find it almost
impossible to make their way to an unfamiliar place.

Jean was disturbed by the afternoon's visits. She had
met two women her own age who had none of the
advantages working people had won for themselves over

the past fifty years. Mrs Elliot was, like herself, a mother and a part-time worker. She earned more because of her education, yet only a thin line separated her from that bleak poverty, that isolation. She too had been deserted by her husband to whom she had given the most energetic years of her life. And if she wanted another job, and she would certainly be needing one when this project ended, her age would be sure to count against her. People think older women are just rubbish, she reflected bitterly.

The bus turned onto Westminster Bridge and as always her heart lifted at the sight of the river. Parliament was all lit up, the buildings like a fairy castle reflected in the water. How beautiful, she thought, the bus turning among the crowds, the cars streaming past, the solid stone buildings solemn in their show of power.

'It was like coming into London from another world,' she said to Sara as they drank whisky and hot water later that evening to keep away the cold. They had formed the habit of sitting up with hot toddies to review the day. When Don came in, picking his way over the floor cushions on which they were sitting, to make himself a cup of cocoa, he laughed at what he called their 'alcoholic vices'.

'Oh yes,' he commented, 'medicinal, I suppose,' and disappeared into his room.

'I mean it,' said Jean. 'It's another world across the river. Or maybe it's just this wave of anger I feel when I think about those women.'

'How do you mean?'

'Well, I just feel so like them. More so than with the women at the conference. I feel it at gut level, even though I know they probably looked on me as some kind of loony social worker. I didn't experience them or myself like that, just this anger that women should have to live such lives.'

'Yes.'

'You know, the social worker told me that when Mrs Elliot had been here about eight years, the poverty and the babies dying and her son so far away and out of reach, she went in for some kind of voodoo magic, lit fires in the

95

council flat, burning their furniture. They put her in a mental hospital for a few years. Karen and Sharon were taken into care. That was when her husband left her. Think of her feeling so powerless and not knowing how to cope.'

Sara saw that she was close to tears. 'Let's have another hot toddy. Come on, Don already said we were alcoholics and anyway, it's Saturday tomorrow.'

The difference between Mrs Elliot and me, thought Jean the next day as she swept her carpet and tidied her room, isn't just the money, although it makes a lot of difference, but that's not what gives me the sense of power I sometimes have. The difference is Sara, the way we talk, the way we can work things through together. It's tied up with the feeling of not being alone, of being able to change things, even when there aren't demonstrations or conferences.

'Let's go to Compendium this afternoon,' she suggested to Sara. 'There may be some new books in the women's section. You know, those new novels from America.'

Chapter Thirteen

The girls' group became for Jean the most exhausting event of her week. Ten girls had decided that they would become members of the group, and turned up regularly each Friday afternoon, although, as if to stretch Jean and Paula's confidence to the limit, they always arrived late, and also, for some inexplicable reason, together. Paula once laughed at this and said she wondered how they managed it, as they all came from different estates. Perhaps, she said, they met secretly around the corner in order not to arrive alone in the project.

The group was a kind of see-saw of power. The two women wanted to talk about the futures ahead of the girls, the choices open to them. Jean wanted to tell them how she had expected marriage to be her most important achievement, and how disappointed she had been. She wanted to share with them her new knowledge that she liked living on her own in spite of the fears she had had. The girls didn't want to talk. They brought records which they played at ear-splitting levels on the record-player, they demanded to be taken out, to the circus, to the fun-fair, to the cinema. They knew that they wanted more from their lives than they were getting and saw the Friday meetings as a way to explore all the things they had never had the money to visit.

For this reason there was tension between the women and the girls, but there was also an unease among the girls themselves. Some of the very shy girls had joined the group after all. Two girls, one dark and one fair, would walk shyly into the room each week and sit quietly through the noise and the chaos, their silence making a mute demand on Jean to see to their needs as well. Jean and Paula spent hours discussing how they could reconcile these very different claims on their attention and especially how they could keep Sharon and her friend Joy, who turned out to be very large and dominating, from deciding what would happen each Friday afternoon.

'We spend all our time discussing how to deal with Joy,' complained Paula. 'It's as if even when she's *not* here she still wants all our attention!' Amanda never came to the group, but Jean wondered whether it would have pleased her. The noise and the suppressed violence would probably have driven her away.

'I want to make a cake,' Sharon would say, but give up half way because she came across something she couldn't do and was afraid to continue. 'You finish it,' she would order Helen, who was docile and wouldn't refuse, but who resented it because it was so like her role at home.

Jean talked about the group to Sara. She would come home on Friday evening and sleep through until Saturday fternoon, her body needing to relax after the previous day. Sara, who worked more regular hours during the week, would go to the market and return home with her basket full of fresh mushrooms, apples, pears and tomatoes, so that the mews would overflow with the colour and smell of fresh grown vegetables and fruit. The two women had taken over much of the running of the household: Don was away a lot, he had met another woman who also made shoes and he sometimes spent weeks at a time with her. Mark too was often absent, his course kept him busy and he had a group of friends he met every weekend.

So Jean and Sara often found themselves alone on a Saturday afternoon. They would talk together or walk in the park where the air was now autumn cold, scented by the golden leaves which drifted down under the trees as they wandered past the lake or sat down on the benches to watch the ducks. Dave no longer visited the mews very often and Sara no longer talked about him, just as she didn't talk about the abortion. She shut these thoughts away and instead involved herself in her work, where she had joined the union and was a representative for the workers in the basement. She was now doing battle with the administration who wanted to give smaller pay rises to the women in the post and duplicating room than to the rest of the staff. The women were fighting this, they could see that their work was considered less important, women's work.

'At the meeting on Thursday afternoon, we all wore dungarees,' laughed Sara. 'We didn't plan it, it just happened.'

'So they wouldn't see you as weak women?'

'Yes, something like that, although until I looked at the others I hadn't consciously realised what I was doing when I got dressed. We were all surprised.'

'Do you remember the joke in *Spare Rib*, when someone said that all feminists wore dungarees and smoked roll-ups and lived in rooms with the walls painted white?'

'Yes, it's funny. I suppose we are stereotypes even if we don't want to be. People look at us and the way we dress and decide – women's libbers.'

'I met a youth worker at the project the other day who said that the minute he met me he felt I was too dominant, that I made him feel he must do what I said and he resented it.'

'Well, I wish they would feel that at work. But we'll fight, don't you worry. I want to be strong, not weak. I don't care what they think of me as a woman. I'm a worker too, and they'll soon find out they need me if I withdraw my labour. The whole place would come to a standstill without the printing and the mailing.'

They were strolling next to the lake; a young man was sitting under a group of chestnut trees playing a guitar and singing a sad Spanish song. The two women stopped to listen, the music changing their mood. As the shadows lengthened and the sunlight weakened, Jean shivered and drew her coat closer round her body.

'Let's go. I'm freezing,' she said, and they walked back past a few stragglers in the park, a man with a small dog on a lead, a woman on a bench coaxing a squirrel to eat out of her hand.

During the week, Jean was very much on her own. She would sleep late and read a lot, and shop for the other people in the mews, who went to work earlier than she did, and came back after she had left for the youth club, or a discussion at the workshop, or to visit a friend. She was making friends with the women on the estate across the road and with a group of women she had met in the women's movement. They had squatted a large house together which Jean helped them to paint. She went dancing with them at a women only disco in an upstairs room of a run-down pub. But she spent most of her weekends with Sara. Their lives seemed complete now, yet there were large areas they did not talk about: their sexuality, their loneliness. These feelings were still too raw for Sara, and Jean preferred to concentrate her emotional life on her work and on her political discussions. As the weeks passed and the cold weather set in, Londoners spent more time indoors, the afternoons darkened early and the trees through the mews windows were a delicate tracery of black branches against a pale sky by day or a dark, reddish one at night when the low-lying clouds reflected back the lights of the city.

To Jean and Sara the mews felt like a snug, warm burrow, they cooked meals together and when Monica came over to join them, they bought a bottle of red wine to celebrate. Sara asked women from work to eat with them and Jean also had women friends who would drop in and who would sleep overnight on the cushions in the long room because it was too cold or late to go home. They wore badges which said:
Sisters unite
Abortion on demand
Wages for housework.
None of them were wealthy; they were on social security or in badly paid jobs. They wore faded jeans and comfortable shoes which did not break their ankles and in which it

would be possible for them to run for a bus, or from attack. They were aware of what they were reacting against and talked about it with anger:

'Did you see that judgement in the rape case last week – suspended sentence because the judge said it would ruin his career?'

'Well, at least he was convicted. Do you remember the other one where the judge said women and children were habitual liars and their evidence shouldn't be believed?'

Sara had bought a poster which said: 'There comes a time when only anger is love'. She had changed the words to: 'We must be tough in our tenderness', writing in neat black ink over the yellow background. Jean looked at it from the warmth of their refuge and wondered whether they were moving too far away from the ordinary world ever to get back, and felt afraid.

Around the beginning of November, Clive came to the mews to borrow some tea and stayed for a meal, running home afterwards to fetch home-grown grass as his contribution to the evening. He lived down the road in a large house where there were lots of people and where it was quite common to come home to find the kitchen full of strangers. He liked the warmth of the mews, its stability. The two women welcomed him as they welcomed everyone else who came there and he formed the habit of dropping in often to see them, to cook a meal with them or to bring them a bunch of late anemonies or a spray of bronzed beech leaves.

Clive had been an office worker until the heady years of Woodstock and the big rock concerts. Suddenly the new ideas made his life seem ridiculous; he left the office and enrolled as a gardener in a big city park, but even that work was too regular for him. Now he did gardening jobs when he was short of money. He had cut his living expenses down to a minimum and had enough gardens in Hampstead and Belsize Park to keep him in everything he needed. Jean would come home from work and be delighted to find a small bunch of flowers next to her bed. Or he would see her walk up the road past his house and join her for a mushroom omelette late at night, which he cooked while she sat watching him, a cup of coffee in her tired hands.

To Jean, he seemed the opposite of all she was struggling against. In fact, his gentleness seemed to make her struggle irrelevant. While she worked in the drab world of large estates and ugly, repetitive lives, he worked out in the open creating beauty, looking lovingly at growing things, watching a small sparrow finish off the crumbs of his lunch.

'Don't you see,' he would say, 'if everyone would just get into what the world has to offer, there wouldn't be any need for cities and the big businesses would just perish away.'

Even Sara, who had once called him effeminate, accepted him now. 'He's different from other men,' she said to Jean. 'I can't be angry with him.'

The three of them went on a day trip to Kew, sitting on the top of the bus all the way across London. Although they wore coats, it was sunny and windless. They ate their sandwiches outside under a huge beech tree in the wood, searched on a dead tree trunk for late mushrooms, which Clive identified as oyster mushrooms and edible, and which they picked surreptitiously. They wandered wide-eyed through the tall glasshouses where small, brightly coloured birds flew amongst the tropical palm trees, and returned home red-cheeked and tired. Jean marvelled at Clive and Sara as they pored over flower books while she made coffee, and then watched them making beautiful botanical drawings of the flowers Clive had brought to the mews the previous day.

It seemed to Jean that they had been caught in a miraculous bubble which was floating gently through the air. She held her breath and hoped it would never touch ground. She feared that any change in the relationships between them would break this fragile world, so although she looked tenderly at Clive, watching his slim fingers roll a cigarette, or wanted to touch his long brown hair, now thinning slightly, which hung lightly on his dark navy winter coat, she held herself back. It was as if any emotion of hers would be too gross, she should love him as she loved Sara, exquisitely, without wanting anything for herself and she felt exhilarated by the unspoken affection they gave her without her asking.

She talked about it with Sara. 'I don't know why he comes, except that he likes being with us. I don't want to ask more than that. It would seem exploitative, don't you think?'

'He loves you, though,' said Sara.

'I don't even want to speculate on that,' replied Jean. But she had, of course. If he were to love me for only a short while, she had thought, standing in the road, the street lights already on, as she waited for a bus to take her to work. It would be worth it, even if it were the last love of my life.

Would you really bargain with that? she asked herself as she climbed onto the bus, making her way to a seat upstairs by the window where she could see more of the city. Yes, I would, even if it were only for a few months, she replied to herself.

But she didn't say that to Sara. Instead she said: 'How old is Clive? Do you know?'

'About twenty-nine I think.'

'Twenty-nine?' There was surprise in Jean's voice which she hoped would hide her disappointment.

'Yes, I think so, although he does look older. He looks older than you.'

Jean bundled away her doubts about the future along with her hopes. It was enough, she told herself, to accept the present, and it was certainly marvellous to find a man who did not seem to expect that she should be different from what she was, and who gave her as much, even more than she gave him.

She suppressed other doubts as well. Don and Mark had accepted Mark as a constant vistor to the house, just as they accepted all the other people who came in for meals or stayed overnight, but Dave, on one of his rare visits, glowered at him as he sat with Sara reading a story aloud from the *Olive Fairy Book*, which Sara had fetched from her bookshelf. When Jean went into the bathroom to wash up the supper plates, he followed her and sat on the lid of the lavatory seat to talk with her. Now that he was no longer using the mews, but merely visiting it, Jean had developed an easy friendship with him. She liked his warmth, although she knew she could never expect it or rely on it, but when it was given to her, it was something she enjoyed.

'I don't like him, you know,' Dave announced.

'Yes, I can see that.'

'He oppresses me,' he went on, with a vague gesture of his hands. 'I get this feeling.'

'Do you think you are jealous? That Sara takes too much notice of him while you're here?'

'No. It's something else. It's the things he says. That mystical stuff oppresses me.'

'I know what you mean. I feel like that sometimes too and then I feel dreadful, as if I'm too sharp and unbending. He is really a good person, all the way through, you must believe me.'

'Well, anyway, I've got to go. I must catch a train at eleven. Conference in Newcastle tomorrow.'

Jean was glad that she was to be spending a few days with her mother. Jeremy would be already there. He was coming down from Warwick to see her. Although he had been to visit the mews one brief afternoon, he was busy doing research into wind power and was totally absorbed in his work.

It would be a relief also, she felt, to get out of the mews and see what she really wanted. The closeness of their three-sided relationship and the sexual excitement that Clive generated in her was making it difficult for her to think.

'I'll be up early tomorrow,' she said, going back to Sara and Clive. 'I'll see you both next week. Have a good Sunday.'

Chapter Fourteen

Jean always felt excited when the train neared London. First the station names — Surbiton, Wimbledon — then a glimpse of the river (time to put on her coat), then she could see Big Ben and the train pulling up at the platform, Waterloo. She was returning on Monday evening, the train she had been on would take home today's commuters, travelling back again in the December dark. She was carrying a large bunch of honesty which she had spent all afternoon cleaning, the silver disks, light as paper, reflecting the bald station light. As she waited to show her ticket at the barrier, a man passed her with a shout. 'Merry Christmas!' he said, looking with joy at the shining burden in her arms.

Clive was standing under the departures board, his eyes on her. When she saw him she ran towards him in surprise.

'How amazing! How did you know I'd be here?'

'I telephoned you, but your mother said you had already left, that you had caught this train. I missed you, please don't go away again.'

She didn't know what to do. It seemed so important, yet there was no way of marking the occasion.

'I can't believe it. Look, I've this heavy case, it's got all my winter clothes in it. If you buy me a drink, I'll pay for the taxi home.'

The bar was crammed with sullen people, there was nowhere to put the case without getting in someone's way, and the honesty was in danger of being crushed. They raised their glasses to each other.

'Did you have a good time?'

'Fine. My mother isn't too well. She's going to see the consultant next week. There's something wrong with her eyes. Did you really miss me?'

'Yes.'

They were silent in the taxi, holding hands, and still speechless when they got into the mews. Mark was the only one at home and made them tea, but she and Clive couldn't stay apart, they kissed while Mark talked. Jean tried to pretend a conversation, but she was unable to separate herself from Clive. 'Oh,' said Mark, understanding at last what was going on, and left them alone.

Jean had stopped thinking of herself. She responded only to Clive's tall white body, his lean thighs, his back, his small buttocks. She liked the feel of his beard against her face. She closed her eyes to understand his touch better, her skin sparked off a thousand sensations, her mind swooned into love for him. Although he made love slowly, taking time to enter her, she did not orgasm that night, but she clung to him, his body and hers lay close together, and she woke the next morning refreshed as if from the deepest of sleeps.

Although it was late, he slept still. She got up without waking him and went into the bathroom to wash, then returned to dress quietly in the still darkened room. She would have to go to work quite soon; it was almost time for her afternoon session. She had already missed Sara and Mark and Don, who had left earlier. She stepped out onto the roof to look at the bare trees, the ruins seemed so solid in the cold air. She felt new-born.

The friendships in the mews shifted slightly, a change of gear. It became accepted that Clive would sleep there, although occasionally Jean would go over to his room for the night. When Clive came in he would sit next to her and she would move to make a space for him. On the weekend she saw less of of Sara. It was not that they avoided each other, just that in their new excitement in each other's bodies, she and Clive would go to bed earlier. At night there were no more leisurely conversations into the early hours of the morning. And in the mornings he was always there. With her mind on him, Jean felt as if she was moving away from everyone else, but there was nothing she could do to stop herself. Nothing was more real than the times they lay together. She wanted him all the time and needed the reassurance of his desire for her.

A week later when she came home from the girls' group, her face drawn from the strain of dividing her attention between the girls and trying to find out how best to let her energy flow into them, Clive and Sara were sitting together reading quietly. He smiled at her.

'You look so tired. Why do you do it?'

She didn't know how to reply. She had no certainty that what she did made political sense. She knew she was breaking new ground, but how could she say that working with girls was a way of changing the world.

'I want to,' she said weakly.

'You don't, you know. Otherwise you'd look happier doing it. You need to change your head, live in a different dimension. Don't you think she needs a holiday?' he said, appealing to Sara. And Sara agreed.

'You could say you were ill. I can get a van for a week and we could go to Wales. We should go now, before the weather turns really cold. What do you say?'

It wasn't how she usually thought about her work, but seeing it from this quiet place, it did seem as if she was achieving nothing important. She was tired. A week away would be so wonderful, and if they left soon, they could fit it in before all the Christmas fuss. Paula had had a few days off, she could phone her in the morning to tell her what she was planning to do.

'Will you come , Sara?'

'No, I've a union meeting next week. I think you should go though, you need to get away. You have been working too hard.'

That week seemed to Jean a jumble of images, all of them

equally clear, as if they happened together in a bright explosion. They climbed down steep cliffs to deserted sandy beaches, made fires from dried sea holly and bits of driftwood. They woke early in the cold van and went outside into a world which was white with frost, each leaf or frond of fern outlined with a thin cold line. When the sun grew hotter the frost melted and they made breakfast, the smell of bacon and mushrooms mingled with the woodsmoke.

Clive loved nursing a small flame into an efficient fire to cook on. He had brought a blackened frying pan and kettle. Jean had provided the food. They had everything they needed. They ate fish and chips in windy seaside cafes and Jean washed in the van with cleansing cream, or in a pub toilet when they went for pints of beer, sitting in warm dark corners next to a fire, talking about themselves, their lives, their hopes. Jean knew she was being sucked into his life. She aspired to be like him, living close to the earth, the growing world, picking wild mushrooms or brewing clover and yarrow into strange aromatic teas.

One night when they were sitting in the dark next to a carefully contained fire burning in a cleared patch of ground, waiting for the kettle to boil, the traffic police stopped to see who they were and what they were doing. They had not found a suitable place to park the van that night so they had drawn up in a lay-by.

The police inspected the fire and seemed satisfied, but they wanted names and addresses. Clive Brown, age: twenty-nine; Jean Gardner, age: forty-three. Clive didn't seem to mind, but Jean did. She felt a sudden cold fear. She was investing too much in him, was leaving herself behind; how could she be sure that she would have anything over when they were no longer together? She did not say this to Clive, it was understood between them that they were only with each other as long as they wished to be. She told herself that she had seen enough of marriage and what it had done to her not to entertain the notion of marriage to him. She didn't want to have that dependence on another person, to see her life as only a secondary existence. She needed more space for herself now, she told herself. Yet the bald police questions frighened her, made her fear for the happiness she had been feeling.

They had stayed over in a farmhouse for a few days with friends of Clive. The men all knew each other, had worked together, and decided to live away from the city. They told Jean that Wales was a place with strong mystical forces and that was why they had moved there. Both the men and the women seemed very tall and strong to her. They wore warm baggy clothes and big muddy wellington boots, their hair streaming over their shoulders, or tied back to keep it out of their eyes. They worked for local farmers, or made jewellery to sell in the market town. One of the women knitted colourful jumpers which she also sold. At night, the men played musical instruments, the guitar and flute, singing wild open songs about the freedom they wanted to live. The women sat with children on their laps, listening.

Over supper on the second night one of the women looked curiously at Jean. 'Are you Clive's lady?' she asked.

'No,' said Jean. 'It's not like that. I belong to myself, not to Clive, but I am a friend of his.'

In spite of her brave words, she wasn't so sure. Is it any different? she wondered. They would return to her room in the mews and their shared nights. She wanted it that way, could not do without him. She watched him in the group of people on the farm, taking pleasure in his lean body, his long white hands. She waited for him to smile at her and to come over to sit beside her. She waited for him to put his arm round her so that she could relax against him. She was losing her grip on her work, was losing her own friends. She had watched Sara become stronger since the abortion, clearer about herself and what she wanted. Now she could see Sara watching her give herself away. They did not talk about it. It was not in the nature of their friendship to interfere in each other's lives.

Winter Spring

Chapter Fifteen

Mrs Gardner was dying. The consultant, a large, confident man with a healthy red face and broad shoulders, looked across his desk at the small, white-haired lady and told her why her eyes were troubling her.

'It's the tumour on your brain. It's interfering with your sight, that's why you are having double vision. Do you want us to operate?'

She looked back at him, drawing up her shoulders into a brave set: 'I'm eighty years old, I don't want to hang on. How long do I have?'

The answer was vague. The growth could be quick or slow; there could be other growths. She had, he expected, at the most two years. He could give her drugs which would slow it down. Perhaps.

Mrs Gardner was thinking of Jean. There was no need to tell her yet; it would only worry her. Perhaps when her job at Waterloo came to an end, she could tell her. It was lucky it was only a temporary job, otherwise it would spoil her chances for promotion to stop to look after a sick mother. What a pity she hadn't found a nice man in London. It would be so pleasant to die with Jean settled again.

She thought about dying. No point in keeping an old body alive. Yet she did hope she would see the roses bloom this summer. And there was that magnolia tree in a warm corner of the cathedral grounds of which she was especially fond, and the huge old wisteria against the south wall.

She walked into the butcher at the corner of her road. 'I'll have half a pound of salmon,' she said firmly.

'That's very expensive at this time of year, Mrs Gardner,' replied the butcher in amazement. 'Do you know how much it costs?'

'Yes I do. I fancy a bit of salmon. Half a pound will do.'

I'll have to get the ramblers pruned quickly, before anything else happens, she thought as she opened her front gate. Already she had to black out one side of her glasses to stop her double vision from making her lose her balance. There wasn't much time left, she knew that.

*   *   *

In London, Jean was always cold. The mews was warm, but when she ventured outside, the wind seemed to sweep down the streets as if down a mountain canyon. There wasn't much snow, a few slow flakes floated past her window one morning, but they didn't settle. There was just this dead, cold wind, which blew bits of grit into her eyes and froze little cakes of spit onto the pavement.

After they had returned from Wales, she and Clive had talked about moving to the country. She had entered his world now, her own grey London life seemed drab in comparison. They would buy a house and work on the land, and perhaps other people would join them. It was an old dream for Clive. 'Why don't we join your friends who are already there?' asked Jean, but he didn't want to do that. He wanted his own place, where he could decide who came in and who didn't. Jean was glad that he said that. She had a vague picture of herself and Clive fixing up a small cottage or coming in from the cold outdoors to a bright fire.

Nevertheless, she was uneasy. Clive never seemed to work any more. He would lie snug in her bed and look at the grey window. 'The ground will be too hard today,' he would say, if he said anything, if he even woke. Jean was always the first up and her little room seemed filled by his sleeping presence. Every morning she felt as if she were pulling herself out of a swamp. Her life had seemed to slow down so much that there was no longer time or space for anything else. At night she clung to him, warming herself on his body, holding him close to her, both of them safe in the rocking ship which was her bed, but in the morning she woke bad-tempered, angry that it was always she who stood up first, who made the bed and tidied the room so that there was room to sit, to read.

She spoke gently to Clive. 'I'm worried about money,' she said, 'if you don't work we'll never save enough to get away.'

He looked down at his hands which were busy rolling a cigarette and then at her. 'You don't understand. It's the weather. You can't garden in this weather.'

'Oh my dear,' she said lovingly, 'I'm sorry. It's not for me to say,' and she came to him and kissed him and stroked his hair while he sat a little sulkily, concentrating on his fingers' expertise. She knew she loved him now more than on the day he had met her at Waterloo Station. She felt committed to him, her body knowing who he was at a level of understanding far beyond words. Yet she also knew that he had changed since that time. He no longer jumped up to make tea or wash the dishes; his energy spent in winning her seemed now to be all used up.

She talked about it to Sara. 'How can I go to Wales with him?' she asked. 'I know him better now, how can I go with this lethargy?'

'Perhaps it's only now,' comforted Sara. 'Maybe it's just the winter, you know how things slow down in the winter. And he's right about the gardening, there isn't much point in going to work when the ground is frosted hard.'

But at eleven o'clock the next morning, Jean looked at his sleeping body in her bed, the room still smelling of yesteray's clothes, last night's sleep. She was dressed and wanted to be alone. 'I feel so oppressed,' she said to him as he turned over to open an eye to her, and she climbed through the window onto the roof to look at the maze. Its magic seemed to have deserted it, it was damp and muddy with rubbish from the surrounding houses dumped in it, as if the debris from the streets had washed up there. It looked suddenly like a city tip. Even Cocaine was not to be seen. He had probably found himself a corner out of the wind.

When she returned to her room, Clive had gone. The bed was made and his clothes had been whisked away. She felt a tremor of fear. I'll go shopping, she thought. I'll visit Walter and Janet. It's an age since I've seen them – or anyone else either.

At the community shop, Walter was stock-taking. 'Haven't you heard the news?' said Janet. 'We've been given eviction notices. The council wants to do up the houses into maisonettes, the ones across the streets are going to be pulled down to make room for that big ICI building. Some of the squatters in the square are thinking of barricading themselves in, but we can't risk it, we've too much money invested in the stock.'

'Where will you go?'

'We're thinking of Bristol. We've friends there and it'll be quite easy to get premises. There's lots of alternative projects going on. Perhaps they'll like our bread.'

Walter came over to them. 'Has Janet told you the news?'

'Yes. We'll miss you.'

'Oh well, you'll be moved soon too, I expect. What about some tea?' he asked, looking at Janet, who left quietly to fetch the cups and tea from upstairs.

Jean stood at the open hearth where a warm fire was burning. She wondered how the council would treat all this lovely stripped wood, the oiled shutters folded against the windows, the pine boards under her feet. A large black and white cat lay in a basket near the heat, suckling four tiny kittens. 'You don't want a kitten at the mews, do you?' asked Janet, as she returned with a tray.

'No thank you. I'll ask Sara though. Clive and I are thinking of moving to Wales, so we're also up in the air at the moment. If we do go, we'll call in to see how you're getting on. When will you leave?'

With the square being knocked down, the dreams of the summer were coming to an end with a vengeance. February is a bad month, she thought as she walked back towards the mews, there seems no hope in it somehow. How is one supposed to believe that it could ever be warm again, or even that the sun will ever shine?

Clive stayed away all day. At first Jean enjoyed the freedom of being alone. It was unusual for her now. She had forgotten what it was like, and sat quietly reading on her bed. Looking up at intervals she could see bare trees and grey sky through her window, but as the day progressed and the window darkened her mind kept turning uneasily to Clive. Perhaps he would never return, perhaps this was the end, two words spoken in anger, a sense of wanting her own space, resulting in an empty desert of loneliness.

She did not remember her old fine anger, that exhilaration which had made her reach out for her own identity. Without deciding to, she had delivered herself into Clive's hands just as securely as if she were married to him. All the love she had carried inside her had welled out to him, enclosing him and her in a world which made no room for any other interests. Her work seemed puny, her friends dispensable. Even her friendship for Sara was not a life choice as her love for Clive had become. And he accepted her love as if it was his due. When she was difficult or short-tempered, like today, he withdrew altogether and she was left with the growing fear that she had lost him, that he would not return, that she would never see him again.

By nine o'clock, Jean was afraid, so afraid that she could not help speaking to Sara about it. 'Clive and I had a row this morning. I'm scared he won't come back.'

'Go to him. Why are you waiting for him? You could at least find out.'

'Do you think so?'

Clive had visitors when she walked shyly into his room. The plates from supper and a few empty coffee mugs were scattered on the floor. One man was playing a flute, gently absorbed, and did not look up when she entered. Everyone was stoned into their own private worlds. Two men and a woman listened silently to the music. Jean went to make herself a cup of coffee and came back to sit unobtrusively in a corner. She would wait for them to go and then talk with Clive.

Clive was standing at the bookshelf with a young man with long blond hair. He had an open book in his hand and had obviously been reading some passages aloud. 'Man, this

Carlos Castanedas was some guy.'

'Yeah.'

'He knew the truth man.'

'Yeah.'

'He could see.'

The musician was packing up his flute. He looked at Clive. 'I'm meeting this chick at Dingwalls tomorrow night. Good music man. You want to come?'

Clive looked at Jean. 'I'll be working tomorrow,' she said. He looked annoyed. 'You go,' she urged. 'Go with them. It'll be good.'

When everyone had left, Jean picked up the dirty plates and mugs and took them downstairs to wash them. There seemed to be an icy wall around Clive which she couldn't penetrate and somehow it was her fault. She thought: Oh, why did I say that to him? I've got no right to speak to him like that. I could lose him now, it'll be my fault, and there's nothing else I really want ever again.

When she climbed the stairs back to his room, she found Clive sitting reading. It was the fourth book in the Castanedas series. They had been sharing it together, but he was ahead of her now and fascinated by it. 'I'm sorry,' she said quietly, standing in the doorway. 'I don't know what came over me this morning. I seem to be so bad-tempered when I wake.'

'OK,' he said.

'Are you still angry?'

'No. You'll learn. You see what it does to me.'

'Can I stay here tonight?'

'Yes.'

He read for a long time sitting at a desk placed in a corner far away from the bed, his book in a pool of light from a fringed table lamp. Clive's room was larger than hers and more opulent, with a velvet hanging on one wall, a vase of peacock feathers on a glass shelf. It was very tidy. The main light hung low over the mattress, which was placed in the centre of the room, but she put it out and lay there, trying to sleep. When he finally closed his book and took off his clothes, she turned to him with so much love that he grudgingly responded.

Chapter Sixteen

Although Jean still talked about her experiences in the girls' group with Sara, she hardly ever shared them with Clive. Her two worlds were entirely separate. She sometimes talked to the girls about her marriage with Stephen or about how she felt as a woman when she walked down the road alone or went into a pub with other women. She did this as a way to open up discussion about the future lives ahead of each girl, to help them to understand that their fears and lack of confidence were not personal to them, but shared, even by those older women who seemed, on the surface, more able to cope. Sometimes, after a good evening, perhaps when Sharon would break out of her self-absorption and show concern for another girl, or perhaps when they had had a pleasant time out together, she would come home triumphant, wanting to talk about how it had been, but Clive rejected her work completely. Having made initial statements about the agony of sex roles, demonstrating by his behaviour that he was not a male heavy who would expect women to cook and clean for him, he had nevertheless lapsed now into a kind of stern superiority which claimed that his dream of living simply in the country would make the problems of city life, and therefore, he seemed to imply, of sexual oppression, irrelevant; they would simply melt away.

'But surely not everyone can do it. Not everyone has the choice. Karen and Sharon don't have the choice,' argued Jean.

'We have to show the way. Others will join us. That's why we need a base, a place. We can make these choices happen.'

Clive was vague about how they would get started or when they would go. Jean supposed they would leave after her work ended at Waterloo, she was already packing up in her mind. She had a little money left in her bank. She didn't know if Clive had any, but she suspected it wasn't much. She left such plans to him. Perhaps they could rent a caravan to begin with. Their holiday in Wales had been so wonderful. She had a vision of a small meadow with a stream running through it, the blue sky above them. Clive was part of this vision, he conjured it up for her like a magician bringing beautiful silk scarves out of a golden ring. She believed in the reality of the illusion, but in doing so she lost the confidence she had gained by being critical. It seemed wrong to doubt what she was being given. It would, she felt, be churlish or ungenerous. Clive, she argued with herself, had given up all ambition and material comforts, so how could she hold back?

Sometimes her old clear anger would return, and such moments were like life buoys in the emotional morass in which she was trapped, although at the time she did not see them like that, experiencing them as moments of deep pain.

Donna Russell was fifteen, turning sixteen. She was a tall, neat girl, sometimes surly, but energetic and lively; she would grumble if she was told that they would be staying at the centre for the afternoon, for she was greedy to be taken out in the city, to the ice-rink, to the circus or to the cinema. She was not talkative, but when they went up to the West End, she clung to Jean's arm, talking fast and rather incoherently about the National Front. 'They're coming for me, watch out, look, there's one over there, oh god, he's coming closer.' Jean comforted her and tried to protect her from her imagined fears. She also knew that Donna's terror was not grotesque, that she had every reason to be afraid, and she tried to make herself large and powerful to put Donna at her ease.

Donna was one of the few girls in the group who attended school regularly. She was hoping to take several CSE exams that coming summer and to look for a job armed with these qualifications. One evening, when it was almost time to go home, she showed Jean a letter. It was from the headmistress of her school and it was addressed to Mrs Russell.

'On Thursday, 10th February, after the second break, Donna was unforgiveably rude to a teacher and has refused to apologise for her behaviour. You will understand that under the circumstances we have no alternative but to suspend her. Her case will be discussed at the next meeting of the school governors on the 10th March. In view of her persistent refusal to apologise for her behaviour, her suspension will continue until that date.'

'Oh god!' said Jean. 'What happened?'

'She called me names so I called her names back.'

'When was that?'

'We was coming in from break and someone pushed her. I don't know who it was, but she grabbed me and said it was me and I must apologise.'

'And then?'

'And then I said it wasn't me and she bloody well wasn't getting me to say I was sorry when I ain't done nothing and she'd no right to say it was me.'

'And you were suspended for that?'

'Yes. Silly cow.'

Jean was silent. Donna was obviously upset. It was enough that she had shown the letter; she was asking for help.

'And your CSEs. How are you managing?'

'I can't do much at home.'

'Have you done your mock exams already?'

'Yes.'

'Did you pass?'

'Yes.'

'Oh damn! they make me so angry. Your whole future depends on those exams and now they suspend you just two months before you take them. Are you seeing Sue Crawford, your social worker, about this?'

'Yes. Me and my mum are going round there to her office next Tuesday.'

'Would you like me to come too?'

'I don't mind.'

'All right, I'll come. What time? Three o'clock? I'll phone up beforehand to ask her. Oh Donna, I am sorry. You don't deserve this.'

'I know.'

The following Tuesday, Jean waited with Sue at her office. It was a new experience for Jean, this friendly, yet impersonal place where social workers received their 'clients'. Sue made her a mug of coffee as they sat talking about Donna and about the group.

'Do you think we could get her to apologise?'

'I don't know,' replied Jean. 'Why should she? It seems a hard thing to ask. It's incredible to me that the school can care so little about her future that they will suspend her just at this time.'

'I know,' sighed Sue. 'There's a funny headmistress, and they've quite a lot of difficult girls there.'

'Donna isn't difficult. She seems perfectly keen to learn and I've never seen her nasty to anyone. I don't know why they have trouble with her.'

'Well, I'll see what I can do. Perhaps we can get Educational Welfare to help. I wonder where they are, it's already half an hour over the time we said.'

But Donna and Mrs Russell didn't come, although Jean and Sue waited another quarter of an hour.

'Could we go round there? Perhaps something's wrong,' suggested Jean.

'All right. It's really against social worker rules, but we might as well.'

Sue drove Jean the few blocks to the house. It was strange being in a car. Jean was so used to public transport, to waiting for buses and then walking, that she was surprised to find herself drawing up in front of the very house they were to visit. The street was a terrace of older houses, the front doors raised by a few steps, the houses all with a friendly aspect, far less forbidding than the estates she had called at when first contacting the girls for the group. Paula had seen Donna then, this was the first time she had been to Donna's house.

'I hope they're in and that they answer the door,' she said nervously.

In the event, Donna came quite quickly to their knock. It was Sue who spoke. 'Hello Donna. We'd been waiting for you, but we thought maybe there was something wrong. Is your mother here?'

Donna said nothing, but turned to lead them up the carpeted stairs to the next landing. They met Mrs Russell on the stairs, she was placing a plastic basin to catch a drip of water from the ceiling.

'I'm sorry not to have come to your office, but I'm waiting for the maintenance man from the council. I've got this terrible leak. I've been at them for six months to come round and they said they'd come today. Look at the wall.'

When Jean touched the wall, she found that it was saturated with water as if it were organic. 'Don't you get mould on this?'

'Yes I do. I have to wipe it off every day. Look at the carpet. I can't think what it's doing to the electricity and the woman downstairs keeps having trouble with her lights.' The carpet was soggy with water. It was a pretty dark blue but completely soaked.

'Come in. I can't keep you standing here.' Mrs Russell led them into a large front room with two windows, both with net curtains and long drapes. The room was bright and cheerful with lots of objects to dust, everything sparkling clean. There were coloured photographs in silver frames, pottery ladies in long dresses, lampstands with frilly skirts and brightly coloured pictures of tropical beaches with palm trees in the setting sun. Jean sank into a well-upholstered red arm chair. She wondered what Mrs Russell would make of the mews, and thought how shocked she would be at the dirt and mess she lived in. Sue and Mrs Russell sat on the sofa facing her. Donna sat on an upright chair near the door.

'You heard about Donna then?' Mrs Russell asked Jean.

'Yes, I'm so angry. Donna doesn't make trouble. I can't see why this has to happen to her.'

'She stays at home all day now. I've sent her sister away because of the damp in the house, it's bad for her chest, but I'm keeping Donna here. She is trying to work. She watches the TV school programmes in the mornings.'

'Will she be allowed to take the exams?' Jean asked Sue.

'I don't know. I'll have to find out.'

'I've been telling her that she'd better apologise, that maybe that'll do the trick, but she won't,' said Mrs Russell looking over at Donna who sat glum and silent on her chair while the grown-ups discussd her. There was a small tear on her cheek, but she brushed it away and said nothing.

'Don't you think you could do that?' asked Sue.

'I didn't do nothing, why should I apologise? It was her fault.'

'I know,' said Sue, 'but maybe if you did, they'd let you go back.'

'Why should I?'

'Oh Donna,' continued her mother, 'they won't let you back to school if you don't. They say so in the letter.'

'It's the teacher should apologise, not me. I didn't do nothing wrong. I never pushed her. It's not justice.'

'Justice?' Mrs Russell flashed into fire now and for the first time Jean saw her as a woman, not merely as Donna's mother. She was tall and good-looking, but her eyes had dark circles under them. 'Justice? When do you ever get justice? You're asking for the moon, my girl. Look at me. I work all day at the cash desk for that Mr Coolidge, and no overtime pay although we often have to stay late and never once even a bonus for Christmas. And look at your father, him with a good business now and me with not a penny, and I spent years helping him build it up. Did I ever see anything of it? Justice? Girl, you're just crazy.'

She settled back into the sofa. The room waited.

Jean broke the silence. She knew that nothing could really follow what Mrs Rusell had said, but they were there for Donna and needed to give her the push which would get her to act, even if it was against her principles, even if it was an entirely cynical geture. Better indeed that it should be, there was no other way.

'Why don't you just do it, not for them, but for you. You play their game.'

Donna said nothing.

'I'll give you a box of Maltesers.' They were Donna's favourite sweets. Jean felt frivolous saying it, but somehow there was no other way to let her see that it was in her own self-interest. It did the trick.

'All right. I'll do it.'

Everyone relaxed now. Mrs Russell talked about the council and the leak and how many times she had been to tell them, but nothing had been done. It was clear that no one would come this afternoon either. Sue said that she would try to get into contact with the school and perhaps Jean could write a letter about Donna and how she behaved in the group to show them that Donna wasn't a difficult girl. Nothing was solved and Jean left with a troubled feeling, as if she had let herself down.

She never heard what happened about the house, as she didn't visit Donna again at home, but, in spite of Donna's defeat, the school did not take her back. She was so close to sixteen that no one from the educational authority bothered to find her another school or help her to sit the exams. She still came regularly to the group but talked not about school but about finding a job and trying to save money because her father had promised her a trip to America in the summer.

A few weeks later as Jean stood in front of the grimy main-line station, waiting for the bus to take her home from work, she tried to imagine what else they could have done that afternoon, and knew that they had failed. It was no wonder that Donna was wary of grown-ups, that she used them to give her treats and trips out, rather than confide in them. She had seen how little they could really give her. Justice? That wasn't a word left in her vocabulary.

Chapter Seventeen

Sara watched Jean give herself away, but said nothing. She accepted that she would have second place in Jean's life if Jean were to 'fall in love'. Yet it hurt her that Jean could so easily relinquish the closeness they had shared. Why, she wondered, is it that friends are less important than those people we are fucking? Even though, she continued bitterly, thinking of Dave, the physical relationship seldom lasts very long?

Her love for Jean, however, encompassed that understanding. She could see herself doing the same thing. In fact, in her all-absorbing relationship with Dave she knew that she had left herself with no props of friendship to hold off despair. The irony was that Jean had come into her life at the very time when she had so badly needed a friend who would choose her, not Dave. She was someone outside her life with Dave. Yet now she saw how Clive claimed the same attention from Jean which Dave had claimed from her. He expected Jean to be home when he called, to provide him with food, even though he wasn't a member of the household. One evening when Clive came in, Sara was cooking for a friend she had invited. 'I'm sorry, there isn't enough food tonight,' she had said with some effort. 'Do you think you could eat at home?'

It was difficult to say because she knew that Clive had almost stopped contributing to the food kitty in the house he was living in. She had heard rumours that they were planning to ask him to leave. They were saying that he no longer gave his share to their communal household. Clive, however, said nothing of this, and Jean, a silent witness to their conversation, watched Clive leave the house.

'I'm sorry,' said Sara. 'I think he should be told that we can see what he's doing. And there really isn't enough food tonight.'

It's all right,' replied Jean. 'I'm bothered about it myself. He doesn't seem to give much any more. It's difficult for me to talk about it to him. I'm glad you spoke.' But as the evening progressed, Jean became more and more nervous and at ten-thirty she excused herself with an apologetic smile and walked quietly out to visit Clive.

There was nothing else said between Jean and Sara, but Sara spoke to Don a few days later. It was he who started the conversation. 'Do you think Jean's all right?' he asked. 'She doesn't look too marvellous. Are they really going off to Wales in a few months?'

'I don't know,' Sara sighed. 'Jean says they are, but Clive has hinted to me that he wants to go on his own. I don't think he's told her yet.'

'You know, I don't like him any more. He used to be such a helpful person, he's changed, don't you think?'

'Yes.'

'It's these heterosexual relationships,' Don commented. My time with Mary is over too. She wanted us to live together and I can't yet.'

'You still seem to be out a lot. I always thought you were seeing her.'

'No. I've met this amazing American, he's an actor. A huge fellow with so much energy. We're talking about doing theatre in the parks in the summer, for children mostly. Pass round the hat afterwards. We've got lots of ideas.'

'Do you love him?'

'I'm infatuated with him. It's not the same as with Mary. I don't feel I have to be responsible to him. There's much less guilt in it. I think I'll give up being with women altogether.'

'And give up the shoes?'

'No, I can't do that, but I want more than just sitting for hours in front of a shoemaker's bench. It's not exciting even if the shoes are fantastic. You know, the ones we make now are selling for a hundred pounds? Not that we get paid that.'

'You'll never be able to stop. It's an obsession. When did you start making shoes?'

'Oh, when I was sixteen, after I had been expelled from school. Why do you say it's an obsession?'

'It's just that you always work as if there's something inside you that makes you. I've got it too – I think. I'm going to do a course in printing next year, get properly trained. I've already written off for the information.'

Sara was feeling stronger now than she had ever been since coming to London. She was looking around her for the first time with a sense of being able to make her own demands on the world. Being a printer was one step forward. There was Dave as well. She hardly saw him now, although the hurt was still there, a kind of emptiness inside her which she was aware of even at her happiest moments. Perhaps it was the power of sex, she thought cynically, the pull of the genitals or even just the feel of another body, skin against skin. I should do something about it, she decided. Why not? At work there was a man she found attractive, he was lively and very much a ladies' man, with dark, curly hair. One day over lunch at the pub, she asked him to the mews. 'I like you,' she said, her heart beating with the fear that he might see how awkward she was at this, how unused to it.

But he didn't notice her nervousness, so surprised at what she had said that he assented quickly. He had always admired Sara's calm efficiency at work, but had regarded her as unapproachable, not the type of bird you could chat up, too much of a women's libber for that, which made him both frightened and intrigued by her offer.

So the mews became a place where individuals merged again into couples. There was Clive and Jean, and now Sara and George. They went to films together sometimes, or for a meal at the local Indian restaurant, but mostly there was little communication between them. George was a smart young man with a sense of style, who found Clive's rough country manners unattractive. He and Sara sat in her room listening to records. He was fascinated by her politics and felt flattered that she had chosen him as a lover.

For her part, Sara despised him. When they talked about what went on at work, he was so completely unaware of her feelings as a woman. There was too much between them that they would have to argue about, too much that seemed to her self-evident that she would have to explain to him. She had aproached him because she needed sex, or that was what she had thought, but their love-making didn't fill her up. There was still that empty space inside her. Without his clothes, he was a disappointing figure, shorter than she had thought him to be and not as stylish. They both knew that this wasn't love, yet he was perfectly satisfied to be with her without any real emotional attachment or respect. She despised him for that too, although she knew she did it herself. At least, she thought, I'm troubled about it.

One Saturday, while she was taking her washing to the launderette, she asked him to go to Compendium to buy her a large and much-discussed book on rape. She had heard about it from Monica and, although it was expensive, it was still in hard back, she wanted it. It was called *Against our will*. George was glad to go. He felt that he could participate in Sara's politics if he bought her feminist books and Compendium wasn't far away. The day was sunny, though cold, and perhaps they would go out together afterwards. He liked being with Sara out of doors, he liked the way she walked, fast and purposeful, unlike other girlfriends he had had who clung to his arm.

But he was disappointed. When he brought the book, Sara said: 'Oh, thanks. Can I look at it? There's tea in the pot if you want some.' And that was all. He paged through the *Daily Mirror*, put on records, wandered through to the kitchen and talked with Jean who was sweeping the carpet. He made more cups of tea and gave them to everyone in the house, but Sara still read on. He even went out into the maze to see Cocaine, who came up to him in a lumbering, friendly way to have his ears scratched. Sara was totally absorbed. He felt at a loose end, dangling. He went out to the house next door where he knew people and talked there, but they were all planning to go out. He hung over the bonnet of a car which someone was servicing in the mews, discussing the problems of its generator, but he got cold and came back inside. Sara ignored him all day. He settled down with a book which he didn't want to read, waiting.

Sara read. She read about rape on the streets, rape in war, rape in slavery. She read about the crimes against women undocumented in the history books or in novels and films. She read about this violence and it clarified her own sense of the violence done to her. It fed her anger. That was what was happening when she walked in the street, that was what social control of women meant. Coercion through violence and the threat of violence. The fear of rape making her seek the protection of a man, making her give up her liberty. It crept into her life, the very fabric of her personal relationships. She recalled how different it was to walk down the street with Dave, and now with George, than it was when she walked alone, or even with Jean. How each man, as if obeying an unspoken pact between them, respected the property of the other, unless they were at war. A property which, once owned, could be used at any time.

And Dave? How many times had she been afraid to refuse him her body? Even when she feared she might become pregnant, she couldn't say no to him because there was always the threat that he would discard her, leave her. Her pregnancy was the result of such an occasion, yet he had blamed her for it, had said that she was trying to trap him. She was the one who had been trapped, for his maleness made him the natural ruler of her world. He claimed her body even at times when her heart was broken because of what he was doing to her.

Each page of the book described the pain and humiliation suffered by women, sometimes in a woman's own words, sometimes just in cold statistics. She was reading about what had happened to women all over the world and it was her own pain. She remembered with anger the day she had returned to the mews to be greeted with Dave's destruction of her life, his visit to her while she was trying to tidy up, the casual way he had waved an arm and shrugged off his own violence, the way he had borrowed her money and used her body, making sure she still belonged to him, that she would not dare blame him for what he had done.

'A sexual assault is an invasion of bodily integrity and a violation of freedom and self-determination wherever it happens to take place, in or out of the marriage bed.'

Jean and George brought her cups of tea which she hardly drank. Later she could hear them cooking in the room next to hers, but it was miles away from where she was. George brought her a plate of food, and she ate a few mouthfuls, but mostly she read and read, the ideas coming at her like recognition, the fury building into a flame, her rage consuming her.

Still later George came to her. He felt hurt. He had waited all day to speak to her and she still took no notice of him. After all, he had brought the book she was now reading. Didn't she want to share it with him? 'Sara,' he said tentatively, a note of complaint in the tone of his voice. 'It's after eleven. Let's go to bed.'

She looked up from her book. Everything seemed to happen in slow motion, both for him and for her. It was as if the room and the two people in it were objects seen from a distance, as in a play. She closed the book and moved her arm in a slow arc as she threw it at him.

'Get out,' she said. 'I never want to see you again. My body is my own. Don't you dare claim it.'

Chapter Eighteen

Clive had started work three days a week in a garden up in Hampstead. He was being paid partly in meals and was often late back. His employers were a young married couple, June and Colin. Clive talked a lot about them to Jean. 'Colin works in the city. He doesn't come home till late and June feels so isolated in the house.'

'What's she like?'

'She's lovely. I feel sorry for her. She's lonely and Colin has treated her very badly.'

'How was that?'

'Well, he's brought other women home and things like that. They're into sex a lot. She's got gold rings in her nipples. She did it to please him.'

'Does that turn you on?'

'Yes, I suppose it does.'

Jean kept her emotions down. Loving Clive didn't mean she owned him. And she loved women too, she didn't want to be competitive with them. June was her sister, even if they had never met. She would love her too, just as Clive did.

Clive came in late when Jean was already in bed. 'I want you to meet June. You'd really like her. What about coming up with me on Saturday when I go to work? They're really cool, you know, and they're having other friends round. It should be a good crowd.'

'Oh, I'm sorry, that's the weekend I'll be away with the girls' group. Remember, we've booked this adventure centre in Kent for the weekend. Social Services is paying a lot of money for it. We'll be riding motor bikes and shooting on the rifle range! I'll tell you what, I'll come up with you the first day after the weekend and then we can really talk, without too many other people around.'

*　　*　　*

The six months with the girls' group was nearly over. Part of what they had planned was a weekend away with the girls and this had been delayed because of the cold weather. Now it was almost time to say good-bye and the excursion had been organised in a rush. Paula and Jean discussed what they wanted for the girls. 'Let's do the most active and daring things we can find. I haven't ever had a chance to do half of what they offer. I want to have go as well,' said Paula.

'Right. But don't expect me to go on the assault course. I'll take charge of the camera and keep on the ground,' was Jean's reply.

So it was that much of the weekend seemed to Jean to be framed by the camera. Even their first encounter with the youth worker who ran the centre, seemed like that. He was sitting in the well-equipped kitchen waiting to welcome them, a large middle-aged man with a slack mouth, his muscles gone to fat. Seeing a minibus full of girls and two women stop at the door of the centre, he banged on the table with his fists like a small boy. 'I want some tea!' he cried. 'Who's going to make the tea?'

'You run this place, why don't you make tea for us? We've paid enough for it,' Jean responded coldly, carrying in boxes of food from the van.

'I want some tea,' he cried again, but this time without conviction and watched them settle in. There was a large sum of money set aside for the weekend and they had bought nearly a hundred pounds worth of food. Such lavishness seemed obscene to Jean, who lived quite sparsely and knew that the girls did as well. The girls couldn't get over it. Joy and Sharon raided the fridge and the cupboard, taking frosted cornflakes and packets of biscuits back to their bedrooms to save to eat later. They were like squirrels stocking up for the winter.

But the five months hard work had paid off. The girls were a group now. They chatted easily together, and with Jean and Paula, they helped each other choose beds and inspected the bathroom, they played table football in the recreation room, cheering each other on. 'What are we going to do now?' they asked and went off to explore the grounds of the centre and the river at the base of the meadow along which the assault course was laid out in a mystifying series of ropes and tree trunks and tunnels which they would be taken over the following day.

Jean watched them and loved them. She watched Donna career round the meadow on a motor bike, screaming because she couldn't find the brakes. She stood in the mud on the river bank, sniffing the damp smell of leaves and moss, watching sunlight filtering through bare branches, and saw how brave Sharon was to trust herself to walk the taut rope high up between tree and tree and then do a terrifying swing back onto the ground. She took photographs of them all, laughing in hysterical fear at Joy who first stood clinging to a tree trunk set across a deep drop over the stream, screaming; 'I'll tell my mother on you!' and then shrugged it off, triumphantly non-committal on the other side, having made it after all.

Sharon and Joy went with her to buy a few things from the village shop. The owner regarded the girls with suspicion. 'Wait outside. We don't want people like you here,' he grumbled, at which they all walked out indignant.

'How dare he!' exclaimed Sharon, hurt.

'Pigs!' swore Jean.

'National Front,' pronounced Joy and they marched back to the centre a little daunted, the green spring day a little spoiled, but not for long.

On Sunday morning they walked to a farm to ride ponies, who were coaxed along by the farm owner and his son. The women sat high up on these strange animals, moving in stately procession round the farmer's fields. There was sunshine and birdsong. Paula had the camera this time and took photographs of everyone; Joy and Donna laughing together, Jean nervous on a stolid horse.

That morning Paula had said at breakfast: 'Jean and I have decided that we want a group discussion before we leave today.'

'What about?'

'About the group and what it means to us. We've never done that before and we want to know how you feel about it.'

'Why?'

'Well, just because we've been together now nearly six months and there must be something we've learned from that.'

'We don't want to,' they said, looking sullenly at each other, suddenly withdrawing from the two women.

'Well, we do. And we're not leaving until we've had it.'

By lunchtime the air was full of resentment. The pony rides had made them late and it didn't help that they were all sick with hunger. No one spoke. The food tasted bland and stodgy, although Sharon and Paula had taken a lot of trouble cooking it.

'It's like a family Sunday dinner,' said Jean to Paula and they giggled.

After lunch they sat in a circle in the recreation room. Sharon wouldn't sit down. She stood in the corner, banging at the table snooker.

'Come on, Sharon,' said Jean. 'We can't start without you.'

'I'm not coming.'

'We're not leaving before this is over.'

'Come on, Sharon.' This time it was Donna. 'Let's get it over with.'

Sharon sat down heavily. 'All right then. Talk.'

'It's just that we've been together now for five months, meeting every week,' said Jean, 'and we've never talked about why we wanted a girls' group in the first place, why we've excluded boys from the group.'

'Well, you did that,' said Donna.

'Yes, I know.' This time it was Paula. 'Do you think it would have been better with men youth workers? Or if we'd had boys in the group with you?'

There was a sort of shuffle through the group and a grudging 'No' from most of the girls. Helen had her hands in front of her face to make sure no one would catch her eye. There was no answer when Paula pressed them to give a reason for their reply. This was hard work. Jean had promised they would spend only half an hour on the discussion and already Sharon was timing them with her watch. The girls had united against them.

'We wanted the group to be only girls because we thought that we would be able to talk better about what we think about being women, about what we want from life, about sex and marriage and the jobs we get,' Jean tried again.

'Look,' said Joy firmly. 'We'll talk about anything you say, but not that.'

'What do you mean?'

'Not that what you said. It's dirty. We won't talk about that. It's not right. You can talk about anything else.' She was a big girl and she drew herself up into a full matronly stance. Jean felt she could see Joy's mother before her and her mother's mother, and her own mother. A long line of strong women, silent.

'But we all do it.' There was a suppressed giggle from Sharon. 'Aren't you going to get married any of you?'

'No.' This time they were unanimous. 'No, we won't get married.' They all came from homes where the father no longer lived with them. They all knew what drudgery marriage had turned out to be for their mothers.

'And love? Don't you think you'll ever fall in love?'

But it was no good. This was as far as they would be allowed to go. Perhaps another day, perhaps there would be another time.

* * *

Jean wondered whether she was really more open about her own feelings. When she was with Clive she hid her pain because she was ashamed of it. She felt it would be wrong to say: 'Commit yourself to me, I want all of you.' When she got back to London she went with Clive to visit June. It was a clear and windless morning, the thin spring sunshine picking out delicate sprays of winter jasmine, the first few blossoms showing on an occasional tree. June's house wasn't opulent, but it was comfortable with a wide terrace facing a small walled garden. June was sitting drawing at the pine kitchen table. She was dressed casually in jeans and sweater, but her clothes looked money. Jean calculated, she's twenty-five I think, I'm glad she's got lines round her eyes, but she smiled when Clive introduced them and said: 'I'm pleased to meet you, Clive has spoken so much about you.'

Jean could not tell whether June was also hiding her insecurity. They spent the day together, pruning untidy shrubs against the garden wall, burning rubbish, drinking coffee and talking. As Clive brought a tray of tea cups and buttered toast onto the terrace, June said to Jean: 'I've never met anyone like Clive before. He's so sensitive and kind. I've never read fairy stories with anyone else before.'

Jean looked at Clive who, to do him justice, looked a little sheepish. It was a long time since Clive had read fairy stories aloud to her and Sara. His behaviour that day reminded Jean of the old Clive. It was as if he was re-running a successful movie. Now he was mending a plug because June had told him she had trouble with the toaster.

'Colin promised me that he would do it ages ago,' said June and Clive clucked sympathetically.

'Did he put up those shelves he said he would?'

'No. He went out instead to see some clients.'

'Don't worry. I'll teach you how to use the drill and then you can put them up.'

'He won't like that.'

'Well, he'll learn from it.'

When Colin came home he parked the car and brought in a bag of shopping and a bottle of wine. Jean sat across from him at the dinner table whilst June and Colin prepared the dinner. For the first time that day the atmosphere was electric with suppressed sexuality. Until his arrival, Clive and June had not seemed to need to touch, yet now it was as if each time they came near each other their bodies sent off sparks of desire. Jean looked at Colin. Did he see this too? she wondered. How did he feel?

She heard her own voice, bright and brittle, laugh and joke. Pretend, pretend, she thought. Don't let anyone see. Be cool. When Clive put his arm around June, Jean caught Colin's eye, Had he seen? Clive put on a record: 'After midnight, we're gonna let it all hang out,' the voice sang. Clive's body swayed seductively to the music. It isn't for me, thought Jean, it isn't even for June, it's for Colin. He wants Colin's woman now, and he wants Colin to know that he has had her.

That morning Clive had told Jean that he and June had 'got it together' over the week-end. Colin, he continued, was jealous, but he had told Colin that it could only make things better between him and June. They had been having 'problems' lately. But Colin had replied: 'The moment I saw you, I knew you'd get her.'

Jean thought about her life with Clive. She felt as comfortable with him as she did with herself. Being with him meant that she had stopped feeling alone. She felt part of the world now that she had someone who loved her. She didn't want to lose that. And she felt also that their time together had made each of them tolerant of the other's frailties, as we are of our own. She was planning a life with him. Now she was seeing once more the Clive who had first wooed her, the energetic non-sexist man who had captured the hearts of those two strong feminists – when was that? It seemed so long ago. At least *that* Clive was known to her. Yet she thought she was sensing something new. Was it right to criticise Clive for fitting in with people who lived so obviously in the kind of style he himself claimed he had rejected?

He was wearing a gold bracelet which belonged to June. He luxuriated in it, aware of its value. June had given it to him to look after, he had said. He wore her dark glasses to protect his eyes from the unusually strong spring sunlight. 'They're Foster Grants,' he said, 'they're worth about twenty pounds.' He was high on their food and their wealth as if that nourished him so completely that he needed nothing else.

On the way home, Jean said: 'You know, you said you thought your relationship with June would make things better between her and Colin, but you put him down all day.'

How do you mean?'

'Well, like saying he hadn't done the plug, or the shelves and was lazy and so on.'

'I know, I can't help myself. I must stop.'

She started on the part of him she was just beginning to see. 'If you want to live away from money, then you have somehow also to give up wanting the good things too, don't you think? I mean all the luxuries. Otherwise it seems to me to be a contradiction.'

'Well, that's me,' was his reply. 'You'll have to accept that.'

It was too much to think about. She lay awake all night wondering if he would rather be with June than with her. June was younger, more beautiful, richer; what could she, Jean, offer?

Chapter Nineteen

The squatters had been evicted from the square. Walter and Janet had long since gone. Others had barricaded themselves in, saying they would not leave without a fight, but the police had arrived in the early morning and the battle was soon over. Now the bulldozers were working on the site and half the houses were down. When Jean walked past she could hardly believe that everything had fitted into such a small space. Had there really been a square there? Was that where Sangito had lived, that gaping hole where the cement pylons were being driven into the ground to provide foundations for yet another skyscraper? 'City blight' Walter had called it.

Her own street was still untouched, but its population had changed. Now most of the people living round her were strangers to her. Clive had been asked to leave the house he was in, they wanted his room for someone else, they resented the fact that he was hardly ever there and did not subscribe to the food kitty. Clive, on the brink of departure anyway, didn't bother to argue. 'Is it cool if I stay with you?' he asked Jean, and she helped him put his things into packing cases and store them in the basement of the house next door. It made little difference to her life, seeming only another confirmation of the permanence of her commitment to him.

So she was taken aback when he spoke to her over a cup of tea in the park cafe. I've been thinking,' he said, 'I think I should go to Wales on my own at first. I want to see if I can make it on my own. It's my old dream.'

In many ways she was glad. This was the old Clive, the one she had fallen in love with, the man who wanted to be self-sufficient, who would camp in a wood and live off the land. He would be using his own energy to survive, not depend on anyone else. She could see him most clearly like that. It was what she wanted him to be and she could not ask where she fitted in.

'I understand. Don't worry, I think it's best too.' She wanted him to be strong and clear and call her to him. But she was filled with doubt. Why should he do that?

She watched him when they were out together, how he talked with other people and came back to her almost grudgingly when they were about to leave for home. She felt empty, uninteresting. She sat quietly with no fire in her. When June came round to the mews, she made her and Clive coffee and brought it to them as they sat sheltering from the wind on the roof, looking at a yellow bush afire, forsythia, which grew in the yard next door. The maze itself was barren, for everything green was immediately eaten by Cocaine. June had a car, a battered MG, which Clive loved. When the three of them rode in it, Clive sat in the back, his hand on June's neck. She purred like a cat.

What was the use? Nothing which is not freely given is worth having, she said to herself.

At the girls' group, the final meeeting was tearful.

'But we told you this was for six months only. They didn't give money for more.'

'Why not? Why can't you come next week?'

'No, it's finished now. We can't.'

'You always do this to us. Give us something and then take it away again. Why?'

'It's not us. Ask John. He set up this project. Why don't you go to his office and ask him? I'll be without a job too now.'

She barely said goodbye. Sharon and Joy and Karen

were in the office, arguing with John. Jean felt too tired to stay. She and Paula hugged each other.

'We'll see each other again. I'll send you a card,' said Paula.

Jean felt broken by all these events. She was without a job, and now possibly without the future she had been planning. She could hear the girls' angry voices in her head. Why didn't she keep the group going anyway, without pay if necessary? Didn't she care? She had meddled in their lives and now was walking out on them. They were right to see it as just another let-down. There was nowhere else for them to go. In the whole borough there was not another group like it. Money from Intermediate Treatment was spent on boys, thousands of pounds went into equipping car maintenace shops, carpenters' benchs, to keep the potential trouble-makers off the streets. The boys, the courts said, were at risk. And girls? They were at risk too, but not a danger to society. When they spend money on us, she thought bitterly, it's just a luxury.

On the way home, she thought about what would happen to the group. John would send them home. Donna would find the kind of job her mother hated doing. Joy already had a boyfriend, was talking, in spite of what she had said on that weekend, of getting married. Nothing she and Paula had said had changed any detail of their lives.

The next morning there was a postcard from Mrs Gardner. The writing was large and untidy, not her usual neat hand.

'Not feeling well. Can you come down?'

Jean threw some clothes into a suitcase. Sara and Mark were finishing a late breakfast, Clive had left early to help Colin and June put up a trellis. 'I've got to go to Winchester,' said Jean. 'My mother's ill.'

'We'll ring you to find out how bad it is,' said Sara. Jean kissed them both. 'I'll bring back plants for the window boxes on the roof. Say goodbye to Clive for me please.' She arrived at Waterloo Station a few minutes after the tain had left. She would have to wait another hour. She hurried to one of the telephone booths. 'I'll be there after lunch, Mother,' she shouted into the phone, the line was bad and announcements of trains arriving and departing made it even harder to hear anything. She hoped her mother would know it was her.

She bought a sandwich and a plastic cup of tea and carried them to the benches near the departure board. A woman with several plastic carrier bags filled with paper made room for her. Jean tried not to look at her, but her eye caught bare legs in old furry boots, two or three livid sores on the calves. Oh god, she thought, I can't bear it. The tea tasted hot, but flavourless, the sandwiches turned to dough in her mouth. Across from her was a noticeboard: 'There is a £10 fine for feeding the pigeons,' it announced. She remembered how her mother would stealthily drop bits of bread for the birds when she thought no one was looking. Her mother needed her and had asked for her help, but how long would it be for, would she ever get back again to her life in London? she wondered. It was time to go through the barrier. It was stupid thinking like that anyway, she told herself as she walked along looking for an empty seat. She hadn't done much to make a life for herself. She was unemployed, dependent on Clive, on someone else, for the future she wanted. She had done this to herself, and now he was retracting, thinking of other, better alternatives.

The house looked the same, yet there was something wrong. It was nearly as clean and fairly tidy, but it had lost its glow. It was as if Mrs Gardner had been absent for a week or two, on holiday perhaps. Even the garden looked as if something was missing, although the daffodils were coming out in a yellow wash all over the lawn.

'How are you feeling, Mother?' Jean asked.

Mrs Gardner had grown thinner and smaller. Her one eye had closed. She told Jean that the doctor had said it was an automatic reaction to the double vision. It didn't look unsightly, merely absent, a lack among all the other absences.

'I feel I look a freak,' replied Mrs Gardner. 'Does it look awful?'

'No. Somehow you carry it off. I wouldn't worry about it if I were you. How do you feel though?'

'It's these headaches. They come right across my head, a kind of –' she passed a shaky hand across her forehead to indicate the area – 'horrible prickly pain. They usually come on in the afternoons. The doctor says aspirins should help, but they don't. I can't bear the headaches.'

'Well, I'm here now. We'll both go to the doctor tomorrow and demand he give you something stronger. I'll make supper.'

The fridge was stocked with food as if Mrs Gardner was preparing for a long seige. There were at least three dozen eggs and six pounds of butter. Jean felt disoriented as she put on the roast and beat up egg whites for a pudding. She was unused to cooking a meal like this. It felt like being married again. How long will I have to stay, she worried. After her mother had gone to bed, Jean sat watching television until late into the night. She hated the artificial sound of the voices, but had no one else to talk to. Her old loneliness was returning. She could see herself sitting alone in this room for endless nights, sharing empty laughter with strangers who could not even know she was there.

The next morning as she was making tea, there was the sound of a fall from Mrs Gardner's room. When Jean opened the door, her mother was lying on the floor straining to lift herself up.

'Wait. I'm coming,' Jean urged as she rushed to her mother's side, holding her up by the arms and shoulders. Mrs Gardner's body was weak and drowsy, her muscles had gone completely limp, and she was unable to help Jean in any way. I'll never make it, thought Jean, but she did and after what seemed an age of pushing and pulling, Mrs Gardner was back in bed. She immediately curled up under the sheets. Jean, who had always imagined her mother to be a big woman, was shocked to see this tiny bundle in the bed.

'What happened?' Mrs Gardner was falling asleep again. 'I took some pills,' she mumbled drowsily. 'Been saving them since your father died. They were very strong, but I didn't take enough. I thought if I took too many, I'd be sick up and they wouldn't kill me.'

'Oh mother, there was no need,' Jean cried out, anguished.

'Yes there was. It's time.'

'I'll make some tea and call the doctor.'

But Mrs Gardner refused to eat anything. In spite of her sleepiness, she was vey firm.

'I've had enough. I don't want food. No.' And she shut her mouth tight and turned away her head.

Jean waited helplessly for the doctor. When he came, he made phone calls and arranged a nursing home. On his way out of the front door, he spoke to Jean. 'Your mother has a large tumour on the brain. It is probably only one among other cancerous growths in her body. She refused, quite sensibly, to have an operation. It looks as if she has also not taken the medicine we prescribed.'

'She's had a lot of pain from headaches.'

'Yes. When she's awake, I'll tell the nurse to give her stronger pain killers. If those don't help we'll put her on heroin. It's quite standard practice for cancer patients. I've told the ambulance to come at three o'clock this afternoon. Try to make her eat a little lunch.'

Mrs Gardner slept. Jean made tea and sandwiches, and woke her, but she still refused anything except a few sips of tea. 'Oh, mother, why didn't you say?' asked Jean, but Mrs Gardner just smiled vacantly and slept again. Jean spent the day hovering around the bedroom door, alternately weeping in short spasms of dry tears, or busying herself with a duster and vacuum cleaner. She looked at her face in the mirror and was surprised to see how white it was. She had developed a rash on her cheek and under her hairline, like a pale pink scar. Perhaps cancer is infectious, she thought in a dull panic.

The ambulance was on time. Two large men in uniform came into the house, carryng a kind of litter, a chair onto which they bundled Mrs Gardner. 'Come on, love,' they said to the sleepy old woman.

Jean stood in the doorway of the bedroom, watching. She felt a rush of anger. They were treating her mother as if she were a child, as if because she was old and sick she was also less than human. They raised their voices as if they were talking to someone who was not only hard of hearing, but also a little stupid, who could not be relied on to behave in a self-directed way.

144

'Put your arms outside the blankets, love.'

Mrs Gardner was still half asleep. She looked to Jean as if she couldn't imagine what was happening to her, as if she hated this invasion of her privacy, yet thought perhaps that it was only a bad dream. She tried to curl up again by pulling her arms back inside the blankets, but they were put firmly outside again. Jean watched her being carried out of the house and into the ambulance.

She picked a large bunch of daffodils to take to the nursing home. She had never been there before, but it was only ten minutes' walk away, a large Victorian brick house with a locked front door. She rang the bell.

Inside, the house was comfortably furnished as if for a family, but it was somehow bigger than a normal house with a public air about it, like an empty guest house with everyone out. Her mother was in a small bedroom upstairs. She seemed to have no memory of having been brought there.

'The nurse is very kind,' she said to Jean. 'Will you be sure and make her a cup of tea?'

Although Mrs Gardner soon fell asleep, Jean stayed for over an hour, sitting in a chair next to the bed and thinking of all the people she would have to ring to tell them that her mother was ill. In the next room another old woman cried out continually for attention. 'Nurse . . . nurse,' she called despairingly, but no one came. The house was very quiet except for the old woman.

On her way downstairs, she was stopped by a plump woman in a starched white uniform, a watch pinned to the bib of her apron. 'I'm Sister Green,' she said, holding out her hand. It was firm and dry. 'I hope this doesn't upset you,' she went on, 'but we have to know. Does your mother want to be buried or cremated?'

Chapter Twenty

The days that followed were given a shape by Jean's visits to the nursing home. She went every morning and in the late afternoons. At first Mrs Gardner was impatient. 'Why don't they finish me off?' she asked angrily. 'It's time now, it's what I want.'

Jean, confused and frightened, tried to be calm and sensible. 'Oh Mother, remember *Lear* — "Ripeness is all." Just let things happen in their own time.' There were no more headaches now. Sometimes the heroin seemed to give her visions. 'I saw a flock of sheep,' she murmured, but sometimes she was surprisingly lucid, almost girlish. 'I challenged the vicar, you know. I said I wanted nothing from a religion whose god demanded human sacrifice. I saw the nurse nod. He didn't have anything to say to that,' and she smiled.

· Although Mrs Gardner had always shown a lively interest in politics and had never missed reading the morning's *Guardian*, Jean found it hard to talk to her about the events that were reported each day. No topic seemed appropriate. Both she and her mother had been wrenched out of their ordinary lives, placed in this moment where they had only this narrow room as their world. Jean changed the flowers as they faded in the vases on the dresing table, and read aloud from *The Oxford Book of English Verse*, which she found on her mother's bookshelf.

'I wrote a poem when I was at Cambridge,' said Mrs Gardner. She closed her eyes and recited it.

> 'Under the clapper bridge tumbles the stream,
>   Now showing brown, now showing white,
>   Here in the shadow, there in the light,
> With a dart and a splash and a transient gleam.
>
> Hills upon round hills about us rise,
>   Patchwork and brown and green; soft sweet rushes
>   Of air; the bustle of birds in the bushes,
> And a shy moor pony with peat-pool eyes.
>
> Rapturous notes from a lark on the wing,
>   You on a tree trunk reading your lyrics,
>   Half-listening I. O poor panegyrics!
> We've been in heaven or Devon this Spring.

We've been in heaven or Devon this spring,' she repeated, still with her eyes shut. Because Mrs Gardner had spoken softly, Jean had leaned forward to catch the words of the poem, now she sat back, silent. There was a bee trapped in the room, she could hear it buzz against the window. Oh Mother, she thought, you never told me, and it has been sixty years since that poem and now.

'I'm going into Winchester today, to buy a copy of W.B.Yeats' poems,' she said. 'There's one that reminds me of you, and I can't find it in *The Oxford Book of English Verse*. It's called *The song of wandering Aengus*.' That afternoon she read it to her mother.

> 'Though I am old with wandering
> Through hollow lands and hilly lands
> I will find out where she has gone,
> And kiss her lips and take her hands;
> And walk among long dappled grass,
> And pluck till time and times are done
> The silver apples of the moon,
> The golden apples of the sun.'

The words haunted Mrs Gardner's dreams. 'Who is the wandering Aengus?' she asked Jeremy when he came. He held her hand and did not answer. Jeremy loved his grandmother more than he loved any other person in the world. When he was little she had made him fudge on his birthday, and as he grew older she remained the one safe place in his world.

Jeremy came to stay a week after Mrs Gardner went into the nursing home. He was on holiday and would be there at least a month. Jean was glad to have him with her, for his presence made her feel less alone. He did not expect her to explain herself to him; they had friends in common. He recognised the change in her, and welcomed it. At night they took turns to cook meals and watched television together.

There was also a visit from Stephen and his wife, now pregnant. 'We're looking over houses in the Cotswolds,' he annonced over tea, buttering another scone. 'An excellent place to retire to, close to Oxford and yet with a flavour of village life. It's a good time to buy now too, the prices will go up again in a year or two, while the property boom is for the present over.' His voice droned on, talking about the new book he was writing, their plans for the summer. Jean caught herself looking at him in amazement. Had he always been so pompous, she wondered. How can she bear it, she thought, glancing at Jeannette, who sat quietly in a cotton smock, knitting, no doubt for the new baby.

Yet it hurt as well. The cosy sound of the word 'We' echoed in her head. There was nowhere to hold on to, no safe place. She tried to look as if it didn't matter, as if she was strong and clear. At least she would make sure they would not see.

She thought about Clive. He had telephoned the day after she had left London. 'How are you?' he had asked and she poured out the events of the day to him.

'It's terrible. My poor mother.'

'Shall I come down?'

But Jean wanted to give her mother her full attention. She deserved that. Everything that had happened had been such a shock for Jean that she needed to listen to her feelings. If Clive were there she knew she would be thinking of him, loving him. She would lose her sense of self in her love for him.

'I'd like you to come down in a fortnight please. I'll look forward to that. How are you?'

June, he said, had left Colin. She was earning lots of money by posing for nude photographs in girlie magazines. Clive's voice sounded proud, almost proprietary. Was it the amounts of money she could earn that impressed him, thought Jean – he mumbled something about five hundred pounds – or was it his right to the body he was showing off to businessmen and photographers?

'I've been going round with her. The men are so terrible, it's hard for her to do it alone.'

'Of course,' said Jean trying to be supportive, suppressing her fears.

The sunny weather made the routine she had fallen into almost pleasant to follow. She was out of doors a lot and enjoyed the daily walks to the nursing home. As the urgency of her illness subsided, Mrs Gardner reached a kind of half-way state between life and death. Often when Jean visited she was asleep and Jean would sit quietly with her until it was time to go. She was eating almost nothing, but drinking sips of orange squash from a plastic cup with a little spout. Jean changed the flowers in her room and watched her withdraw, although if she was awake she always roused herself to smile a welcome, keeping her old sense of kindness towards the world.

Jean found herself dreaming of when Clive would come down. She imagined he would stay with her through this time. She longed to have him with her, to hold her, Perhaps they could garden together, or she could show him the water meadows as she had shown Sara. He had promised to ring on the Monday of the week he was coming down, to tell her what train he was catching, but the phone didn't ring until Wednesday evening. She could hear it when she reached the front door after her visit to her mother. Although Clive knew very well what times she would be at the nursing home, she knew it was him. She dashed to the phone in a rush, her keys in one hand, the front door still open. She signalled to Jeremy to close it as she came through.

'Hello,' She was all out of breath from the hurrying.

'Hello Jean.'

'Oh darling, it's you. I'm so glad to hear your voice. when are you coming?' As soon as he replied, she could hear from the way he hesitated that he was putting her off.

'Listen, that's why I'm phoning. I can't come just yet. There's a lot happening. I'll come down in about three weeks. I'm flat broke too. I've spent all my money,' he laughed. Three weeks! thought Jean. He could put off his support for three weeks! I could die for want of it.

'Jean . . . Is that OK?'

She knew what was keeping him. There was no point in asking for anything from him.

'Don't bother,' she said. Her reply was instinctive, uncalculated, but definite. They inhabited different worlds now. She could read no understanding for her in his voice or in his words.

'Oh,' he said, sounding surprised by the dismissal. 'Well then . . . goodbye.'

'Goodbye.'

She felt ice cold.

Soon afterwards the phone rang again. This time it was Sara. 'Oh my dear, I'm so glad to speak to you.' Even as the words tumbled out, Jean felt the space she was in unfreeze a little. 'I've just broken with Clive.'

'I know. He told me. He was very upset. What happened?' Sara heard Jean try to explain, but for her the issues were different. 'Did you know that he and June were staying in your room?'

'No. He didn't say, but I knew, I think. I knew she was with him. But that wasn't what mattered though.'

*　　*　　*

But it did matter to Sara. She returned to the mews shaking with anger. How dare he do that? she exploded to herself as she extricated herself from the phonebox and walked back. It's just like Dave all over again, she raged. She slammed the front door shut and clumped up the stairs. She wore woollen stockings and clogs and they made a very satisfactory noise on the wooden treads. June and Clive were sitting close together in the kitchen, like two conspirators, Sara thought, tight-lipped. She walked through without a glance at them. 'Clive, I want to speak to you.' She was already in her room by the time the sentence was over. Clive jumped up immediately to follow her, but stood, embarrassed, in the doorway. Sara turned to face him. 'I'm amazed you didn't even ask Jean if you could bring June to her room.'

He was clearly shaken, his eyes already misty with tears. He looked at the floor. 'I thought I had,' he mumbled.

'I don't accept that. I'm going down on Friday for the weekend, and I'll ask Jean to come up soon. I want you and June out of the mews before then.'

'OK,' he said miserably, turning back to June for comfort.

*　　*　　*

But when Sara went down, she took Jean a letter from Clive. 'I don't want to lose you. We shared the same dream,' it said.

'We didn't,' said Jean sadly, showing it to Sara. 'I was beginning to know that. It's why I was so confused. But what do I do now? It seems as if I've lost everything.'

'I don't see why. You could still go to Wales, there's nothing to stop you. We'd all come and visit you.'

But it was no good. She could not go alone. Her imagination had never provided for that. Oh Sara, she thought, it should be you and me. You're the one I'm closest to, who won't let me down.

They were sitting on a bench set against a high stone wall. The river and the watermeadows lay at their feet. There was no one else about. The midday sun glanced off the water. Two swans glided upstream; with their ungainly feet hidden, their progress seemed slow and elegant.

Jean picked up a small twig and drew a circle in the soft earth. 'Look,' she said. 'This is me. Whatever I mean by that. The person I am inside. Or you, or anyone.' Around it she drew another circle, a narrow space between the two lines. 'And this is the space we fill with lovers, the people we sleep with, whom we allow to touch us. Intimate. Those we regard as part of ourselves, somehow joined to us. For me, that was Clive.'

She drew another, larger circle around the other two. 'And this is everything else we do. This is where our identity comes from. Our politics, our work, our friends. For us, it's mostly with women. The trouble is that the small space is often filled by a man – and somehow the two can't coexist. You have to choose, one or the other.'

Sara said nothing.

'And I feel so lonely with this space unfilled' – she pointed to the circle for lovers – 'it hurts. I don't know what to do.'

Jean let the twig drop, and looked hard at the river. Sara, Sara, she thought, don't you understand? I'm asking you to come into that circle.

Sara stood up, her face turned towards the path ahead of them. 'I understand what you are saying. I can't cope with it though. I can't talk about it, it reminds me too much of my own pain, my own loneliness. I'm going to survive this and I want my friends to be survivors too.'

I'm blind, thought Jean. I think only of myself. I can't use her like this.

'I'm sorry. I forgot to see you.'

'No. Sometimes I think that I've discussed everything I feel with you and it's a shock when I realise I haven't, that's all.'

'You don't have to say everything. The only thing I fear though, is that if we need to build walls to survive, no one will get through, ever.'

'I know.'

Jean stood up as well. 'Let's walk.' They passed under an avenue of lime trees, with new leaves, shiny and olive green just coming out. The path continued under huge chestnuts, their knobbled branches ending in large brown sticky buds, about to burst into leaf. A thrush sang. Jean felt like an alien in this landscape; dried up, shrivelled by her separation from Clive. She pulled her jacket tighter around her as if she felt a cold draught coming off the earth.

The path had curved away from the river, now it turned

back. Almost at the water, the two women paused. 'Oh look!'

Before them in a bowl of sunlight, a meadow of marsh marigolds shone bright yellow. They were larger than daffodils, their flowers were open, exotic, with the look of great buttercups, but sturdier, the burnished petals set in clusters on strong green stems, their smooth finish contrasting with a circle of furry stamens at their centre.

There was no wind here, the meadow's shelter had brought forth this profusion. Sitting on the grass close to the river, the world rimmed with gold, Sara took off her shirt and turned her face to the sun. Jean looked at her and wanted to touch her smooth round shoulders, the cleft between her breasts, but she held herself back. It was too great a step.

She was concerned for her friend. 'It's all right, you know. You are all right as you are. It's enough.'

She did not know if Sara understood. Imitating her, Jean turned her face into the sun.

Chapter Twenty One

Jean caught the train to London the following Friday afternoon. 'I'll be back tomorrow,' she said to Jeremy, who looked a little doubtful about being the only person left to visit Mrs Gardner. 'I'll only be away one night.'

It felt strange walking along the park towards the mews, almost like the very first time, when she had carried the map and knew no one. She could not imagine what she would encounter when she got there. Will Clive really be gone? she wondered. I can't face him, she thought. I can't pretend I don't mind. I know I'll just dissolve into tears. Oh, I hope he's not there.

She put her key into the lock. Sara had said: 'I want you to come up next week end. It needn't be for too long, just a couple of days. You need to establish yourself again.'

'I can't bear to see him,' she had replied.

'I promise you, I'll make sure he's gone.'

She could hear the record-player upstairs. It was Joni Mitchell. 'They paved paradise and put up a parking lot,' she sang. Everything seemed entirely as usual, it was only herself who jarred. She was coming to them smelling of mortality. There was too much pain about her person, the pain of a dying, the pain of losing a lover. Her bag bumped against the wall, she could feel herself slowing down as she neared the top of the stairs.

Don was standing there waiting for her. 'I heard you at the door. What's taking you so long?' She felt very small against his tall, wiry body.

'We've been waiting for you,' said Mark after she had greeted him. 'Sara's gone to buy wine. Do you want coffee?'

They wanted her there. It was clear to her. She put her bag down on the floor and sat at the window. 'It's wonderful to be here. The leaves are out again. The green light is back. It's all happened so quickly!'

'How's your mother?' asked Mark, sitting down beside her and handing her a mug of coffee.

'It's hard to tell. The doctors say it could still be a long time. But she wants to die, and they aren't keeping her alive. I've only come up for tonight and tomorrow.'

She was afraid to go to her room. 'Has Clive gone?' she asked awkwardly in the pause that followed.

Mark laughed. 'Just. They were waiting for you, I think. Sara went out and left me with the message that he and June had to leave before you came. They went about an hour ago. They said something about hitching to Wales.'

Jean couldn't ask whether Clive had cared, but she wanted to know every detail of the conversation so that she could sift through it for some comfort. 'What did you say?'

'I said you were coming this afternoon and that you didn't want to see him and that he had to leave.'

'Was he upset?'

'He just said: "OK." And then they left.'

She could find nothing to hang on to, yet in spite of that she felt a burst of happiness. It was so different from when Stephen had left her. Then everything in her life had changed, she had lost her home and all her friends. This time, her friends had wanted her to stay. They had chosen for her and had gone so far as to throw Clive out so that she should be spared more pain.

'I think I'll go to my room,' she said.

The room was immaculate. She had never seen it so beautifully clean. Her books sat neatly on their shelf, the carpet was brushed up, the bedspread pulled straight without a wrinkle in it, the faulty latch on her door had been mended. On the table next to her bed was a small green bead. Was it a peace offering? She picked it up and threw it in the plastic rubbish bag in the kitchen. She went out onto the roof to look at the maze.

The elder trees were fuzzy with green leaves. The cherry was a mass of white blossom. This was her home. She wanted to wrap it around her, hide in it. She picked a few dead twigs off the plants in the window boxes on the roof, greeting them as she did so. She must make sure to bring up some of the foxgloves which had seeded themselves all over her mother's garden.

The wind was cold. She turned back to her room. As she climbed through the window she could hear new voices in the house. A large man in a leather jacket went past her door. His hair was cropped short, he turned when he saw her and stuck a friendly face into her room. 'Hello,' he said. 'I'm Max. I thought this was Clive and June's room. Who are you then?'

Don was behind him. 'That's Jean. It's her room really,' he corrected Max, putting a hand on his shoulder. This was his American friend.

When Sara came in, Jean did not tell her what Max had said, but his words undermined her sense of welcome. June and Clive had shared her bed, sat together talking with the others, helped tidy up after a long evening. It was easy to imagine that she was no longer part of the household. That night she was very small and quiet and excused herself early. When she was undressed, she examined her sheets before climbing into bed. There was no sign of their lovemaking on them, but they smelled of June's perfume. Amber.

The next morning she was woken by the sound of a heavy thump in the maze. The sun was shining on the wall above her bed, it was time to get up to see what was happening. In the kitchen, she found Mark complaining noisily to Sara that the fleas were hatching in thousands and attacking him, that he hadn't slept a wink all night. He had thrown his carpet out of the window and was going shopping for paint. 'I'll paint the floor too, and the walls, what colour shall I buy?'

When Jean was dressed, she volunteered to sweep out Mark's room. He was lazy about dirt; not seeing it, it didn't worry him. Now that it was warmer, the fleas had hatched in the dust. Sweeping is such a lonely job, thought Jean, as the dust spiralled up into the bars of sunlight which filtered through the leaves and in through the window. Tears trickled down her face and she sniffed to keep them back. Sara came in with a mug of tea. 'You'll need this,' she said, 'to keep your throat from seizing up.' She stood at the window, her back against the light and looked at Jean.

'I don't know,' said Jean, trying to wipe away the signs of her crying. 'I feel so lost. Last night Max said,' she choked a little, 'Max said, that I was in June and Clive's room.' She couldn't look at Sara. 'It's as if I don't belong here any more, as if I should go. I know it's silly, especially when you've all been so welcoming.' Her mouth trembled, she bit her lip to keep her face from falling apart.

Sara's words came out as if they had been rehearsed. 'Look,' she said, 'I'll help you, but if you want to be sorry for yourself, I'm not interested.' Jean's face whitened and she went on, her tone a little gentler. 'You must know how I feel. I want to live differently and I want my friends to be like me. We have to live through things like this to be strong.'

Jean's tears dried with the shock.

'I'm sorry to sound so hard,' Sara went on. 'I think I never liked Clive, and I was right about him. You changed when you were with him. I want you to be like you used to be before Clive. You don't have to be so weak. You have friends who love you.'

'Oh god,' sniffed Jean. 'Don't say kind things. I'll just cry all over again and I haven't got a tissue.' She tried to laugh to hide her tears. Sara came over to her and put her arms around her. Jean buried her head in the hollow of Sara's neck.

'I'll be back soon. I'm going to the market to buy vegetables. Shall we do something together before you catch your train?'

'Yes please.' It was settled that they should meet at three and go down town to see *Bugsy Malone*.

'I couldn't take anything serious after that,' said Sara, and Jean agreed, understanding that it had not been easy for her either. She had made it plain that Jean would have to choose between her dependency on Clive and Sara's way. Jean was surprised to realise that she was relieved.

It was like the old times. Saturdays were shopping days and days to look at the books in Compendium. Later in the morning Jean walked along the park towards Camden Town, keeping next to the railings so that she could see into the park. She passed a field of daffodils, now nearly over, and marvelled at the flowering trees. A woman with long straight brown hair wheeled a small girl in a red anorak towards her. The child's face was purple with angry tears. 'No, I want it now!' she screamed. Jean looked at the woman and smiled and the woman smiled back, grateful.

Its amazing, thought Jean, how easily I greet women, how glad I am to pass them and smile. If it were a man, I'd look away. A smile seems something else to them. I'd be afraid of being misunderstood, or rejected.

She stepped across a red splash of fallen rhododendron flowers. She felt taller and taller, her walk turning into a spring, the movement of her body catching her hair and blowing it back away from her face. She passed an older woman, negotiating the pavement with determined though unsteady feet, and smiled at her as well. She felt as if she belonged somewhere after all. Suddenly it happened to you that you could look around and claim some common experience. She had lost that feeling, so concerned with her own intricate game with Clive. Now she could lift her head again and say: 'This is me. Hello. Who are you then?' to the women in the street.

At Compendium she bought books by Simone de Beauvoir and Marge Piercey. She looked at their shiny new covers, smelled the new pages and smiled to herself. Inside them was a world in which she would recognise bits of herself. There would be women in them who thought as she thought, or who felt the same pain. And they would show her the way, make room for her.

She crossed the road to a small cafe for a cup of coffee. From the outside the windows were steamed over. As she entered she could smell the greasy, salty smell of bacon sandwiches. There were long tables with chairs at them. She took an empty seat next to the wall. It was lunch time. The menu for the day was written on a blackboard: roast beef and cabbage with roast potatoes, egg and chips, sausage and chips. She hadn't realised how hungry she was. The roast beef sounded good. When she had given her order, she wriggled out of her coat and extracted her parcel from the pocket. She tore open the brown paper packet. Which one should she read first? She studied the back covers again. The man serving brought her dinner, the brown gravy steamed on the plate piled with potatoes and cabbage and wafer thin slices of dark meat.

A young woman across the table from her stood up to leave. She had short curly hair and a large, grey, knitted jumper. As she moved her chair, she looked down at Jean's books and read the titles. Then she smiled straight into Jean's eyes. This time Jean hesitated. It was too direct to be comfortable. It was as if this woman were saying: 'I know your secret, it's good.' Jean smiled back, but knew she did not match the radiance of the greeting. She had an instinctive need to cover up her books, as if she wanted to keep something of this new world for herself alone. Why? she wondered after the woman had gone.

There was a big clock on the wall. 2.00p.m. It was time to return to the mews. As she waited for the traffic lights her eye caught a flash of orange on the other side of the street. As she crossed, she glanced at the man; he had a dark beard and was looking intently at her. 'Jean! I didn't recognise you! You've got so old!'

'Yes, I expect I have.'

It was Sangito, he turned to walk with her. 'It was a year ago, nearly. I suppose I've got older too.' He had changed. He had filled out; not so much in his actual weight, but in the space he seemed to be taking up. He had gained confidence.

'Yes you have. I wasn't sure about you either. You seem bigger. You look well.' They stood on the street corner, smiling at each other. 'When did you get back from India? Thanks for your card – you remembered the elephants!'

'I've been back a month, but I'm off again soon.'

'Your room's gone.'

'I know. And you? Are you and Sara still together?'

'Yes, but my mother's ill and I'm in Winchester at the

moment.'

It was time to move on.

'I'll give you my telephone number,' Sangito said, 'I'm staying in Finchley. Perhaps you could ring when you're back in town.' She wrote down the number inside *Small Changes*, on the back fly leaf, but she knew she would never call. She was glad of his concern though, wishing him well, glad too of the change in him.

She hurried on to the mews.

About the author

Ann Oosthuizen says about herself: 'I am a feminist who lives in London. I've written poems and short stories which have been published in collections of women's writing. I write because I enjoy it and because it helps me to understand myself and other people. I've been married, widowed, a student, a lecturer, a teacher, a youth worker, a theatre director, a mother, a lover, a daughter, a friend, a grandmother, a publisher, a translator, an editor. Now I've written a novel. I'm half way through my life and want a lot more from it.'

The following collections include stories or poems by the author:

Licking the Bed Clean by Alison Fell et al. (London: Teeth Imprints, 1978);
One Foot on the Mountain, edited by Lilian Mohin (London: Onlywoman Press, 1979);
Hard Feelings, edited by Alison Fell (London: The Women's Press, 1979);
Smile Smile Smile Smile, by Alison Fell et al. (London: Sheba Feminist Publishers, 1980).

Sheba Feminist Publishers

Sheba is a feminist publishing cooperative, formed in March 1980. All our books are available by mail order from Sheba, 488 Kingsland Road, London E8. Please add 45p per volume for p&p. Write for our catalogue of books, cards and posters.

Other books are

Sour Cream, Jo Nesbitt, Liz Mackie, Lesley Ruda, Christine Roche. A collection of feminist cartoons, 2nd edition. £1.75.

The Ten-Woman Bicycle, Tricia Vita. Illustrations by Marion Crezée. A charming story about how women enter a 'man's world – together. Particularly suited to children. £1.25.

Woman and Russia, translated and with an introduction by the Birmingham-based Women and Eastern Europe Group. The first feminist samizdat, published in Leningrad in December 1979 and immediately suppressed. This is its first appearance in English. £1.95.

Smile, smile, smile, smile, Alison Fell, Ann Oosthuizen, Stef Pixner, Tina Reid, Michele Roberts. A collection of feminist poetry and short stories illustrated with drawings by the writers. 'As my moods change from elation to self-irony to depression and back again, I find poems here to comfort and affirm my experiences.' *Feminist Review.* £1.75.

Feminist Fables, Suniti Namjoshi. Drawings by Susan Trangmar. An elegant and subversive collection of stories that rework mythology as it *used* to be . . . they create an uniquely feminist pattern of meaning. £2.25.

Spitting the Pips Out, Gillian Allnutt. As if entries in a notebook, painful, humourous, despairing, hopeful, this collection of poems, prose and wry comments tell the story of one woman's journey towards selfhood. Though the story is autobiographical, many women will recognise it as their own. £2.25.

Loneliness and Other Lovers, Ann Oosthuizen. A novel of changes, heartaches and discoveries as Jean ceases to be 'someone's wife' and builds her own life, for herself. £2.75.

The Great Escape of Doreen Potts, Jo Nesbitt. An irreverent children's book written and illustrated by feminist cartoonist Jo Nesbitt, with sturdy heroine Doreen outwitting everyone in their attempts to marry her off to the stupid prince. £2.50.

For Ourselves, Anja Meulenbelt. A radical new look at women's sexuality (translated from the Dutch). Richly illustrated with photographs and cartoons, the book is a joyful celebration of who we really are, what we really look like, dismissing once and for all the passive Playboy image that has for so long been called our sexuality. £4.50.

Sour Cream 2. A new collection by thirteen feminist cartoonists: provocative, hilarious, thought provoking. £1.75.

Our Own Freedom. Maggie Murray. Introduction by Buchi Emecheta. 'These photographs of women in Africa show that the basic things of life – obtaining water, fire, shelter, the care of the young and the sick – are almost entirely done by women. These are the basic necessities of life and yet there is little or no compensation to the women who do them. Because they are unpaid, such tiring and boring chores are called 'women's work'. These words come from Buchi Emecheta's introduction to Maggie Murray's photographs of women in Africa. £3.75.

Girls are Powerful, edited by Susan Hemmings. A collection of radical writings by young women from *Spare Rib* and *Shocking Pink* magazines. The pieces in this collection are written by young women from seven to twenty-two, but they contain ideas which will open up discussions between women of all ages – perhaps for the first time. They burst through the notions of what young women can and can't think – to change us all. £3.75.

Rocking The Cradle: Lesbian Mothers, Gillian E. Hanscombe and Jackie Forster. This book looks at the many different ways in which lesbian mothers conceive and bring up their children against the background of a hostile society, and suggests that the way of life of these women has significance for everyone's future. The women interviewed here are but a small group of pioneers – but what they have done, and what many others are continuing to do and say presents a powerful challenge to the nuclear family as the basis of western society. £3.50.

Everyday Matters – New Short Stories by Women. The stories we have chosen for this book have one thing in common: they do not sit comfortably. Each in its own way questions or resists the story we were all brought up on – the one that told us how we feel and what we want and who we are. The stories are varied, provocative, sometimes violent, occasionally humourous. Many are by women who have never published stories before. We hope this book is a beginning for a new wave of women writers. £3.50